Ashton vs. Ashton...vs. Ashton?

The rivalry between two factions of the same wine-growing family is heating up in the valley. While Spencer Ashton is steadily building a wine empire with his popular Ashton Estate Winery label, his children from his previous marriage are gaining on him with their award-winning boutique wines from Louret Vineyards. It is a well-known fact that Spencer Ashton refuses to have anything to do with the children he fathered with Caroline Lattimer, so this reporter is thinking there is more than sour grapes fueling Louret's success!

But if that wasn't enough to turn the Napa Valley into a drama worthy of

Hollywood, rumors are that Spencer Ashton has *other* children from yet *another* marriage hunting him down. A handsome rancher has been spotted at the Louret Vineyards getting cozy with his half siblings—and possibly plotting their father's empire's demise? Like fine wine, this story needs time to develop its full potential—so stay tuned!

Dear Reader,

Silhouette Desire is starting the New Year off with a bang as we introduce our brand-new family-centric continuity, DYNASTIES: THE ASHTONS. Set in the lush wine-making country of Napa Valley, California, the Ashtons are a family divided by a less-than-fatherly patriarch. We think you'll be thoroughly entranced by all the drama and romance when the wonderful Eileen Wilks starts things off with *Entangled*. Look for a new book in the series each month…all year long.

The New Year also brings new things from the fabulous Dixie Browning as she launches DIVAS WHO DISH. You'll love her sassy heroine in *Her Passionate Plan B*. SONS OF THE DESERT, Alexandra Sellers's memorable series, is back this month with the dramatic conclusion, *The Fierce and Tender Sheikh*. RITA® Award-winning author Cindy Gerard will thrill you with the heart-stopping hero in *Between Midnight and Morning*. (My favorite time of the night. What about you?)

Rounding out the month are two clever stories about shocking romances: Shawna Delacorte's tale of a sexy hero who falls for his best friend's sister, *In Forbidden Territory*, and Shirley Rogers's story of a secretary who ends up winning her boss in a bachelor auction, *Business Affairs*.

Here's to a New Year's resolution we should all keep: indulging in more *desire!*

Happy reading,

Melissa Jeglinski

Melissa Jeglinski
Senior Editor, Silhouette Desire

Please address questions and book requests to:
Silhouette Reader Service
U.S.: 3010 Walden Ave., P.O. Box 1325, Buffalo, NY 14269
Canadian: P.O. Box 609, Fort Erie, Ont. L2A 5X3

ENTANGLED
Eileen Wilks

Silhouette® Desire

Published by Silhouette Books

America's Publisher of Contemporary Romance

Special thanks and acknowledgment are given
to Eileen Wilks for her contribution to the
DYNASTIES: THE ASHTONS series.

This book is dedicated to my fellow Desire authors—those on the loop,
and especially those who participated in this continuity series.
You've been a delight to work with. Desire authors are a great bunch,
giving and supportive and maybe a little crazy. I'm glad to be one of you.

 SILHOUETTE BOOKS

ISBN 0-373-76627-0

ENTANGLED

Copyright © 2005 by Harlequin Books S.A.

This edition published by arrangement with Harlequin Books S.A.

® and TM are trademarks of Harlequin Books S.A., used under license.
Trademarks indicated with ® are registered in the United States Patent
and Trademark Office, the Canadian Trade Marks Office and in other
countries.

Visit Silhouette Books at www.eHarlequin.com

Printed in U.S.A.

Books by Eileen Wilks

Silhouette Desire

The Loner and the Lady #1008
The Wrong Wife #1065
Cowboys Do It Best #1109
Just a Little Bit Pregnant #1134
Just a Little Bit Married? #1188
Proposition: Marriage #1239
The Pregnant Heiress #1378
Jacob's Proposal #1397
Luke's Promise #1403
Michael's Temptation #1409
Expecting...and in Danger #1472
With Private Eyes #1543
†*Meeting at Midnight* #1605
Entangled #1627

Silhouette Intimate Moments

The Virgin and the Outlaw #857
Midnight Cinderella #921
†*Midnight Promises* #982
Night of No Return #1028
Her Lord Protector #1160
†*Midnight Choices* #1210

Silhouette Books

Family Secrets

Broken Silence
"A Matter of Duty"

*Tall, Dark & Eligible
†The McClain Family

EILEEN WILKS

is a fifth-generation Texan. Her great-great-grandmother came to Texas in a covered wagon shortly after the end of the Civil War—excuse us, the War between the States. But she's not a full-blooded Texan. Right after another war, her Texan father fell for a Yankee woman. This obviously mismatched pair proceeded to travel to nine cities in three countries in the first twenty years of their marriage, raising two kids and innumerable dogs and cats along the way. For the next twenty years they stayed put, back home in Texas again—and still together.

Eileen figures her professional career matches her nomadic upbringing, since she's tried everything from drafting to a brief stint as a ranch hand—raising two children and any number of cats and dogs along the way. Not until she started writing did she "stay put," because that's when she knew she'd come home. Readers can write to her at P.O. Box 4612, Midland, TX 79704-4612.

THE ASHTONS

Frederick Ashton **m** Patricia Winston

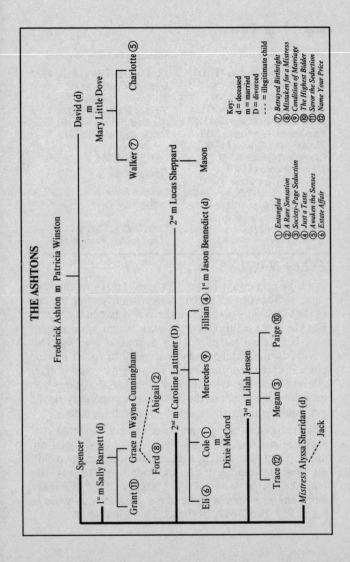

- Spencer
  - 1st m Sally Barnett (d)
    - Grant ⑪
    - Grace m Wayne Cunningham
      - Ford ⑧
      - Abigail ②
  - 2nd m Caroline Lattimer (D)
    - Eli ⑥
    - Cole ①
    - Mercedes ⑨
      - m
      - Dixie McCord
    - 3rd m Lilah Jensen
      - Trace ⑫
      - Megan ③
      - Paige ⑩
    - Mistress Alyssa Sheridan (d)
      - Jack

- Jillian ④ 1st m Jason Bennedict (d)
  - 2nd m Lucas Sheppard
    - Mason

- David (d)
  - m
  - Mary Little Dove
    - Walker ⑦
    - Charlotte ⑤

Key:
d = deceased
m = married
D = divorced
- - - = illegitimate child

① Entangled
② A Rare Sensation
③ Society-Page Seduction
④ Just a Taste
⑤ Awaken the Senses
⑥ Estate Affair
⑦ Betrayed Birthright
⑧ Mistaken for a Mistress
⑨ Condition of Marriage
⑩ The Highest Bidder
⑪ Savor the Seduction
⑫ Name Your Price

Prologue

Nobody expected the church to be full. At eleven-thirty on a rainy Wednesday morning in Crawley, Nebraska, most folks were at work. But the postmistress was there, and the druggist and his wife, and the banker with his wife sat in their usual pew. Many of the county's farming families were represented, for the families of the bride and the groom were farmers.

And, of course, the Mortimer twins sat in their usual spots—sixth from the front on the center aisle. Flora and Dora hadn't missed a wedding in this church for fifty-five years. A little rain couldn't dampen their enthusiasm.

"Doesn't young Spencer look handsome," Flora whispered.

Her sister snorted. "Handsome is as handsome does. You can't tell me that hellion would be up there waiting for his bride if—"

The postmistress turned around and gave them an admonishing look.

"Don't you look at me that way, Emmaline Bradley," Dora said. "Francis is still on 'Rock of Ages.' No reason we can't talk when she's still on 'Rock of Ages.'"

Flora tugged on her arm. "Look. They're seating Spencer's father," she whispered. "He doesn't look very happy about the wedding, does he?"

Dora sniffed. "Frederick Ashton hasn't been happy since he was weaned. Got two moods, that man—mad and madder. What Pastor Brown was thinking of to make him a deacon…well, that's beside the point."

Lucy Johnson, on the other side of Flora, leaned closer. "At least Frederick made sure his son did right by poor Sally."

Flora bobbed her head in agreement like a chicken pecking at the dirt. "Poor Sally. I can see why she fell into temptation. That Ashton boy is so…so…"

"Handsome," Dora finished dryly. "I'm not so sure Frederick did Sally any favors."

"Oh, Spencer's just young," Lucy said. "A touch on the wild side, maybe, but so was my Charlie before we married. And we've been together forty-two years now."

Emmaline Bradley turned around again. "Shh!"

Flora flushed, Lucy's lips thinned and Dora didn't notice. She was frowning at the back of Frederick Ashton's head three rows up. There had been rumors that the man used a heavy hand with his sons. He was big, burly and domineering—the kind who liked to say, "Spare the rod, spoil the child." Dora was sure neither Spencer nor his brother, David, had been in danger of being spoiled.

Francis struck the opening chord of Wagner's "Bridal Chorus." *Here comes the bride...*

At the back of the church, Sally Barnett pressed a hand to her unhappy stomach. The satin wedding gown felt cold and slippery.

"Butterflies, sweetheart?" her father said.

More like nausea. But Daddy looked so anxious...surely Mama was right. Spencer would settle down once the babies came. She summoned a smile. "I'm nervous," she whispered.

He patted her hand. "You're supposed to be. This is our cue, honey."

Together they stepped out in the stately slow march that would carry them up the aisle to where Spencer waited. Sally's skirts swished over the carpet and her heart pounded and pounded. She clutched her bouquet so tightly it was a wonder she didn't squeeze it right in two.

Spencer looked so wonderful in his tux. So what if they'd had to rent it? She'd told him over and over that didn't matter...except that it did. To him. He was hungry for things, for the trappings of success. But she understood why. He'd grown up hearing his mother whine about how little they had, how much better things would have been if his father had sold the farm years ago. He'd come to believe that happiness came from things, not people.

She'd show him differently, she promised herself as her father released her and stepped back. She'd be such a good wife to him that he'd never regret this day.

Her heart turned over when Spencer took her hand, just as it always had for him. He didn't love her. Not in the deep, aching way she loved him. But she'd be patient. She'd teach him how to love.

Nausea forgotten, Sally's face shone as she listened to the preacher repeat the familiar words. Her young groom stood tall and straight beside her.

Spencer glanced at Sally. *Look at the stupid bitch smile,* he thought. *Thinks she has me trapped, doesn't she?* The selfish cow had gone crying to her daddy when she found out she was pregnant, and he'd tattled to the old man…. A trickle of cold sweat ran down Spencer's spine.

"Do you, Spencer Winston Ashton, take this woman to be your lawful wedded wife?" the preacher said. "To have and to hold…"

Frederick Ashton was the one person in the world Spencer feared. And however much lip service Frederick paid to the Bible, his real god was his standing in the community. He'd made it clear that Spencer wouldn't be allowed to tarnish that.

"…for richer, for poorer…"

Maybe Sally had won for now, but not for long,

he promised himself. He was destined for great things. He'd always known that.

"…and in health, until death do you part?"

"I do," Spencer said solemnly. Someway, some-how, he'd find a way out of this dead-end town, out into the wide world waiting for him.

One

Napa Valley, California. Forty-three years later.

Dixie turned off the highway with "Cowboys from Hell" blasting away on the stereo—her notion of motivational music. Who could succumb to nerves with Pantera singing about cowboys from *way* down under coming to take the town?

Her palms were damp on the steering wheel.

She'd missed the light the most, she thought as she pointed the nose of her Toyota down the little county road. Seasons took sharp turns in New York. She'd enjoyed that, jazzed by the way winter hit with a howl and a slap, knocking autumn flat on its face. California's seasons jostled for position more politely, one blending into the next in a watercolor wash rather than the charcoal ultimatums of the North.

But the light… January light in the Valley didn't bounce around with the flat, frenetic energy of summer, but smoothed itself around tree trunks and buildings, settling on roads and earth with a visual hum.

She was looking forward to painting that light. And that's why she was here, she reminded herself as she slowed. She had a job to do. If she could settle a few ghosts while she was at it, well and good. The silly things had started tugging on her sleeve after she returned to California. It was time to look them in their pale, wispy little faces and get on with her life.

The arch over the entry was tall and wide, a graceful cast-iron curve with replicas of the property's namesake vines twining up its sides.

She was here. Dixie took a deep breath and turned onto the driveway leading up to The Vines.

The house lay directly ahead. She took the curve to the left, heading for the winery, offices and tasting room, housed together in a large, two-story building with a roof that made her think of a Chinese peasant's peaked hat. She pulled into the parking lot in a car crowded with ghosts, shut off the ignition and sat there a moment, absorbing the changes…and the things that had remained the same.

Then she retrieved her hat and her purse, checked on Hulk and opened the car door.

The air smelled of earth and grapes. The scents slithered past her conscious mind and plopped into the swampy goo of the unconscious, splattering her with memories.

Not sad memories, though. Loud, laughing, sometimes angry, but not sad. That's what made this so hard. She took a deep breath and let the ghosts slide through her, then stepped forward.

"Dixie!" A slim young woman in a cream-colored suit stepped out on the porch. Her hair had undoubtedly started the day in a sleek knot at her nape. The sleek was long gone, but most of the knot remained. She hurried down the steps. "You're late. Was the traffic bad? What did you forget? Where's your cat?"

Laughing, Dixie caught her friend up in a hug. "Traffic sucked, I won't know what I forgot until I can't find it and Hulk is asleep in his carrier. God, you look great!" She stepped back, looking Mercedes over. "Skinny as ever—they'd adore you in New York—and I love the wispies." She flicked one of the curls frantically escaping bondage. "But that is one boring outfit."

"We can't all dress like *artistes*." Mercedes' mouth tucked down and she shook her head. "Not that I could pull off an outfit like that, anyway."

"You like it? I call it my Beach Blanket Bimbo look." Dixie had changed her mind and her outfit five times this morning, finally deciding on a what-the-hell combination of yellow vintage capris and matching halter top with a Hawaiian shirt in lieu of a jacket. The oversize sunglasses and straw hat were more sixties than fifties, but Dixie wasn't a purist.

Mercedes laughed and started for the building. "But that's just it. You look very retro chic, not like a bimbo at all."

"Well, this is the wrong era for you," Dixie said, falling into step beside Mercedes. "I'm the one with a body straight out of the forties or fifties. You'd look great in flapper clothes—long, lean and sophisticated."

"I am so not the flapper type."

"You're wearing a button-down oxford shirt with that suit, Merry. You need help."

Mercedes held a hand up, half laughing, half alarmed. "Oh, no, you don't. Do not help me. I'm not up to it right now."

"Hmm." Dixie stepped up on the porch and looked around. Eleven years ago this had been a smaller, less stylish building. "Someone does good work. The expansion is invisible—it looks like it was always this way. Now show me your lair."

"If you mean the tasting room, it's through here. We're talking about a possible remodel—Jillian's idea."

Dixie tipped her head to one side as she stepped inside. Mercedes was tense, which was weird. *She* was the one whose stomach had every right to be doing the bubble-bubble-toil-and-trouble bit. "Hey, this is nice." She took her hat off and pushed her sunglasses on top of her head, looking around.

Lots of exposed wood, subdued lighting, great views…nice room, yes, but it suffered from split personality. It couldn't make up its mind whether it was rustic or modern. "What did you have in mind for the remodel?"

"Nothing's decided yet, but we want to unify the look, tie it to the theme of the promotional campaign." The tense set to Mercedes' shoulder didn't ease. "The offices are upstairs. Eli's out in the vineyard, so I'll take you to Cole." She headed for a door at the back of the room at a good clip.

Dixie didn't move.

"Dixie?" Mercedes paused with the door open, looking over her shoulder with a frown. "Are you coming?"

"Not until you tell me what has you wound tighter than a cheap watch. And don't pull that princess face on me," she warned. "It won't work."

"I don't know what you're talking about."

"You've turned polite," Dixie observed. "Always a bad sign. What is it? Is Cole upset that you hired me for the illustrations?" The flash of guilt on Mercedes' face made her exclaim, "He does know, right? Mercedes?"

"Not...exactly."

Dixie closed her eyes and put a hand on her stomach. Yep, things were churning around nicely in there. "Am I going to be fired before I start?"

"He can't do that," Mercedes assured her. "We've got a contract, and he and Eli gave me full authority to hire you. That is, they didn't know it was *you,* but I told them all the places your work has appeared, and they were eager to sign you on."

"And here I was afraid you'd grown risk averse," Dixie muttered, opening her eyes. "What were you thinking?"

"That Louret Winery needs you for our new ad campaign. You're the best."

"I won't argue with that," Dixie said, not being one to underestimate her talent. "But it doesn't explain your vow of silence."

"Do you have any idea what it's like to have your two big brothers for bosses?" Mercedes demanded. "I did not want to waste time arguing with Cole. Come on, Dixie. I know this is a little awkward, but it's not like you're really shook. You?" She grinned. "A tornado wouldn't rattle you."

Shook, no. Pit-of-the-stomach scared…yeah, that was about right. "Cole's face ought to be an interesting sight when I walk in."

Mercedes laughed, relieved. "I'm looking forward to it. And then I'm ducking."

"Thanks. You've made me feel so much better."

Behind the tasting room was a short hall with doors leading into the winery proper and stairs to the office area. Not luxurious, Dixie thought as she started up the stairs after Mercedes, but several notches above utilitarian. It looked as if the winery was prospering.

Eleven years was a long time. What was she afraid of, anyway?

That he hated her.

She put a hand on her stomach again. It had been a long time, yes, but Cole was not a tepid man. He ran hot or cold without lingering much in the temperate zone…though most people didn't see that, fooled by the glossy surface.

Cole did have shine, she admitted. But so does a new calculator.

At least he used to. Maybe he'd gotten fat. Mercedes hadn't mentioned it, but Dixie hadn't exactly encouraged her to talk about her brother. "Hey, Merry," she said as she reached the top of the stairs, "has Cole been putting weight on?"

Mercedes gave her a puzzled look. "I don't think so. Why?"

"Ah, well. Can't win them all." However this turned out, she could take comfort in one thing. Cole wouldn't have forgotten her. "Here," she said, digging into her pocket. "After you cut and run, you can go get Hulk out of the suvvy and put him in my room."

Mercedes accepted the keys. "Um…suvvy?"

"SUV sounds ugly. Suvvy sounds cute."

"Suvvy. Right." Mercedes shook her head, smiling—and impulsively reached out and hugged Dixie with one arm. "I'm so glad you moved back. Sorry for the reason, of course, but glad to have you close again."

"Me, too," Dixie said quietly. "On both counts. Well." She ran a hand through her hair, straightened her shoulders, and said, "How does that poem go? 'Forward, the Light Brigade! Charge for the guns! …Into the Valley of Death…' I can't remember the rest."

Mercedes grinned. "Something about 'cannons to the left of them, cannons to the right.' I'm pretty sure Cole doesn't have any cannons in his office." She turned and rapped smartly on the door on her right.

"I notice you're not disputing the Valley of Death part."

Mercedes ignored that and opened the door. "Cole, our artist is here. Shannon's sick, so I've got to man the tasting room in twenty minutes. I thought you might show her around."

"I'd be happy to," said a smooth, almost forgotten baritone. "As soon as I…" His voice trailed away as Dixie stepped in behind Mercedes.

He hasn't changed. That was her first thought— and it was quite wrong.

Cole was still lean as a whip with mink-brown hair cut short in an effort to tame the curl. He had neat, small ears set flat to the head, a strong nose and straight slashes of eyebrows. But the face that had been almost too good-looking eleven years ago had acquired character lines that rubbed off a bit of the gloss.

Then there was the way his mouth was hanging open. That was definitely different. She liked it.

Dixie smiled slowly, hardly noticing when the door closed behind Mercedes. "Hello, Cole."

Cole's face smoothed into a professional smile. "Welcome to The Vines. As I was saying, I'd be glad to show you around…as soon as I've killed my little sister."

Dixie burst out laughing. "And here I'd been thinking you'd be all cold and businesslike."

"And I know how you feel about businesslike. I'll try to avoid it." He gave her a thorough, up-and-down appraisal that stopped an inch short of insult. "You've always tended to run late, but eleven years is excessive, even for you."

She shook her head. "You aren't going to fluster me that way."

"I can try."

Time to switch topics, she decided, and glanced around the office, which was ruthlessly neat everywhere except for the big, dark-wood desk. A spotted canine head poked around the corner of that desk, brown eyes looking at her hopefully. "Oh!" She bent, smiling. "Who's this?"

"Tilly. She won't let you pet her."

"No?" Challenged, she held out her hand for the dog to sniff—and the animal cringed back out of sight behind the desk. "She is timid, isn't she?"

"That, yes. Also neurotic and not too bright," he said, reaching down to fondle the animal Dixie couldn't see. "Tilly's scared of storms, other dogs, birds, new people, loud noises—you name it, she's afraid of it."

Dixie moved around to the side of the desk so she could see the dog. "She's some kind of Dalmatian mix?"

"That and greyhound, the vet thinks, with maybe some plain old mutt mixed in. I found her on the side of the highway about a year ago."

"How in the world did you get her to go with you if she's scared of everyone?"

He glanced down at Tilly, his smile amused—and slightly baffled. "She seemed to think she'd been waiting for me. I stopped, opened my door, and she jumped in."

Dixie shook her head. "She *is* female."

"But not my usual type." His crooked smile hadn't changed—a downtuck on one side, uptilt on the other, as if he were wryly hedging his bets. "All right, Tilly, that's all. Lie down." Amazingly, she did. He looked back at Dixie. "Are you waiting to be invited to sit down? By all means, have a seat."

Dixie thought that the dog seemed just Cole's type—obedient. Consciously virtuous, she forbore to mention that as she sat in the chair in front of the cluttered desk.

So far so good. The tug in the pit of her stomach was mostly memory, she told herself, a response to remembered passion. It had nothing to do with the man in front of her now. "You've done wonders with Louret Wines."

"Eli is the wonder worker. I'm just the bottom-line man. How's life been treating you? You're looking good."

"My life's been full of the usual ups and downs, thank you. How's yours?"

"Busy. You've made a name for yourself. Congratulations."

A laugh sputtered out. "This will teach me to make a big deal out of things. You wouldn't believe how I'd built up this meeting in my mind. Now, after only a couple of quick jabs, we're exchanging polite compliments."

He quirked an eyebrow. "You're disappointed."

"No. Well, maybe a little." She rolled her eyes. "It's not as if I wanted to be treated to that frigid way you have with people you don't like. You can do cold better than the North wind's granny."

Something flashed in his eyes, but his smile was easy. "I'm a warm, lovable guy these days. Mellow."

That made her grin. "I'll believe that when I see it."

"You'll be here a few days, I understand."

"Poking my nose into everything. That's how I work."

"Hmm." He leaned back in his chair. "You've been compared to Maxwell and Rockwell—not in terms of style, but recognition. I'm wondering how we can afford you."

Dixie let herself look amazed, which wasn't hard. She'd had no idea he'd paid attention to her career. "Didn't you read the contract?"

"For some reason Mercedes wanted to handle everything herself," he said dryly.

"Well, you're buying reproduction rights to my paintings, not the paintings themselves. They'd cost you a good deal more." She planned to give one to Mercedes, but that was friendship, not business.

"So you're not doing this as a favor to Mercedes?"

She shrugged. "That's part of it."

At last he stood. "Would you like that tour now?"

"Let's go."

* * *

Cole waved for Dixie to go down the stairs first, which left him looking at the top of her head. It shouldn't have been an enticing view, but her hair had always fascinated him. Dirty blond, she'd called it. Sand colored, he'd thought. A dozen shades of shifting sand falling fine and straight, like sand poured from an open hand.

"Mercedes will have told you in general what we're looking for," he said as they reached the short hall at the bottom of the stairs. "We're planning a series of ads in some of the upscale magazines and want a painterly look for them, nothing high-tech or mass-produced. We want them to convey the hands-on, personal quality of our wines."

"She did." Dixie had a slow smile, as if she liked to take her time and enjoy the process. "She also said you gave her a hard time about some aspects of the concept."

"You can see who won. You're here, even though it's winter—not the best time for pictures of the vineyard."

"But I'm not painting the vineyard. I'm painting the people."

"She said something about that, but I don't see how a picture of Eli fondling the grapes will sell wine."

"She also said you don't listen to her." Dixie shook her head. Her hair swayed gently with the motion. "There are thousands of good wines out there. Yours may be the best, but how do you show that in an image?"

"Wine, grapes, the vines themselves—they're strong images. A good artist could make them memorable."

Her eyebrows lifted. "I could paint you a picture of grapes that would make teetotalers weep for what they're missing. But everyone's seen beautiful pictures of grapes. One more, no matter how well done, won't identify what's unique about Louret. Your ads shouldn't sell wine. They should sell Louret."

"I'm familiar with the idea of branding," he said dryly. "But why pictures of people?" He'd heard Mercedes' reasons—and they were good, or he wouldn't have signed off on the idea. He wanted to hear Dixie's take on it.

"Because with a boutique winery, it's all about the people. You've established yourself with your pinot noir and merlot. Your cabernet sauvignon wins awards routinely. But the reds come from *your* grapes, your soil, unlike the new chardonnay. You want people to understand that they aren't just buying great grapes when they buy a bottle of Louret wine. They're buying Eli's nose and a sip of your mother's heritage."

His eyebrows lifted. This didn't sound like the passionately impractical rebel he'd once known. "Either you've gotten into wine or you've done some research."

"Wine does come up when Mercedes and I talk, but yes, I've done research. I paint quickly, but I spend a good deal of time researching my subject before I start."

"What happened to your art?" he asked, suddenly curious. "The noncommercial stuff, I mean."

She shrugged. "The art world is intensely parochial. If you aren't playing in whatever stream is fashionable, you aren't doing 'significant work'—which means being part of the dialogue between artists, other artists and art critics."

"You used to like the avant-garde stuff."

"I still do. I just don't want to play in that stream myself. I want to do representational art—which is only slightly less damning than doing commercial art. Which I also do, obviously." She chuckled. "An instructor once told me that I have the soul of an illustrator. He did not mean it as a compliment."

"Some bastards shouldn't be allowed to teach."

"No, he was right. Of course, I think of Rembrandt as a superb illustrator, too." She grinned. "I've never been accused of false modesty."

Or any other kind, he thought, amused. Pity he found that so attractive. "You don't find it, ah, stifling to your creativity to work on the commercial end of the spectrum?"

"I'm in a position to pick and choose my jobs these days. I have a good deal of artistic control, and I don't take work that doesn't excite me."

Yet she'd accepted this job…and for less money, he suspected, than she usually charged. A favor for a friend? "You're excited about wine?"

She leveled a long, thoughtful look at him. "Are you going to give me that tour, or not?"

"By all means." He pushed open the nearest door.

"This is the bottling room. Randy handles things here."

Dixie hadn't changed much. She still had a body that could make a man beg, and a smile that suggested she'd like it if he did. And she still drew people to her, male and female alike. For the next hour, Cole watched her charm everyone she met.

Randy fell easily, but he was young and born to flirt. Russ, who was foreman at the vineyards, wasn't much more of a test—he was older, but he was still male. The real challenge came when she met Mrs. McKillup. The crotchety old bookkeeper actually smiled. Cole didn't think he'd seen her do that over anything less important than a new spreadsheet program.

And none of it bothered him. That realization gusted in while he was watching her twist Russ around her little finger. Jealousy wasn't even a smudge on the horizon. It wasn't there at all.

The lightness around his heart grew with each introduction. He hadn't needed proof that he was over her. Once he knew she'd really left him he'd set out to forget her, and had done a damn fine job of it. Some men enjoyed sighing over a lost love. Not him.

But he hadn't known for sure he was past the jealousy, not until today. He could stand back and watch her flirt, appreciate her body and her easy laugh, without sinking into that old swamp.

Maybe he wouldn't kill his sister.

"You let me have a look at your laptop," Mrs.

McKillup was saying as they prepared to leave her to her numbers. "I suspect you just need more memory. Very easy to install, if so."

"Thanks." Dixie smiled ruefully. "I'd really appreciate help from someone with a functioning left brain. I think mine gave up on me years ago in disgust."

"Not much doubt about the health of Mrs. McKillup's left brain," Cole said when they were on the stairs, headed down. "You could cut yourself on it."

"What an image." She grinned as they reached the bottom floor. "She reminds me of my third-grade teacher. The woman terrified me."

"You weren't showing any signs of fear."

"Oh, I decided a long time ago that it's easier to like people, and you know how I hate to waste energy. It's also much more interesting."

And that, he understood, was the root of her charm. It wasn't about getting people to like her. It was about liking them. Which might be what had gone wrong with them—there'd been too much she hadn't really liked about him.

The flash of anger surprised him. He squelched it. Old news. "Some people aren't easy to like."

"True. And a few aren't worth the effort, but you can't know that until you've tried." She opened the door to the tasting room. "I'd better get the rest of my stuff unloaded. I'm not sure where to put it, though."

"Mother has you in the carriage house. You'll remember it."

She stopped with the door open and aimed a glance over her shoulder at him, her face quite blank. "Yes," she said after a moment. "Yes, I do."

The carriage house was set away from the main house—not far, but enough to offer some privacy. On that long-ago summer, he'd been living in the big house still; Dixie had moved in with her mother after graduating while she looked for work. She'd come to visit Mercedes one day.

By that night, she and Cole had been lovers. They'd met at the carriage house often. Made love there.

She gave a little shake of her head, half of a smile settling on her mouth without touching her eyes. He couldn't decipher the emotion there. "You going to give me a hand with my things, or do you need to get back to work? I warn you—I don't travel light."

"No problem. I love to flex my muscles for the girls."

Her gaze wandered over him, head to toe, a spark of mischief replacing the unknown emotion. "Got a tank top? It would be so much more fun to watch you flex in one of those."

The rolling rise of heat didn't surprise him. She was a woman who'd always provoke a response in a man, and when she looked at him like that he'd have to be dead not to respond. But the strength of it was unwelcome. "Still playing with matches, Dixie?" he asked softly.

"I run with scissors sometimes, too."

She was far too amused. For now, he'd let her get

away with that. Later, though… Dixie wasn't a woman for the long haul. He knew that, and he knew why. But she was hell on wheels for the short term.

"Let's go exercise my muscles," he said lightly, leaving it up to her to decide what kind of exercise he had in mind.

Two

"**Y**ou're driving an SUV."

"I prefer to call it a suvvy." Dixie did not care for the look of unholy delight on Cole's face. She opened the door on the driver's side. "Were you going to ride to the carriage house with me, or would you prefer to tote and flex over there on foot?"

He climbed in, looking around. "I could have pictured you in a Ferrari. Or something tiny and fuel efficient with a bumper sticker asking if I've hugged a tree today. But an SUV?" He shook his head, grinning. "It's so soccer mom."

"Nothing wrong with soccer moms." She hit the accelerator a little too hard. "I do a fair amount of work on location. I needed to be able to haul around my equipment, not to mention the Hulk, and this *is* the most fuel efficient suvvy on the market." And why was she so defensive, anyway? "So what are you driving these days? A shiny new Beamer or a Benz?"

"A five-year-old Jeep Grand Cherokee, eight cylinders, standard," he answered promptly.

"An SUV."

"Yep."

She glanced at him—and they both burst out laughing. "Were we really that shallow before?" she asked. "Arguing about cars as if it mattered." She shook her head, remembering.

"Speak for yourself. I wasn't shallow. Just stupid."

Not stupid, she thought. Obsessed, maybe. Ambitious, certainly. Grimly determined to outdo the father who'd walked out on him, to prove that he and his family didn't need Spencer Ashton in any way—definitely. Dixie had understood that. She just hadn't been able to live with it.

The carriage house was located just behind and to the east of the main house, but to get there by car they had to drive well past the house and circle back, passing through a portion of the vineyards and a small grove of olive trees. Even in January, the trees were picturesque with their knotty limbs and gray-green foliage, and the hummingbird sage and licorice plants beneath them were green.

The grove was even prettier in the summer, surrounded by rows and rows of lush vines, Dixie remembered wistfully. But perhaps it was just as well she was here in January.

"So why a suvvy?" she asked lightly as she came to a stop in front of the small stucco building. "You can't need to haul things around that often."

"Not as much these days, no. But for a while I was. I bought a small cabin a few years ago and have been working on it ever since."

"A fixer-upper?" she asked, surprised. The Cole she'd known had wanted the newest and best of everything.

"You could call it that, if you're feeling generous." He opened the door.

She got out. "What would you call it?"

"Pretty decent now. Uninhabitable when I bought it. I wanted the land, the view, and planned to tear down the cabin and put up something new and shiny. Somewhere along the line, though, I got hooked on power tools. The cabin's been my excuse to use them. Do you need *all* of that carried in?" He gestured at the piles in the back.

She grinned. "I warned you."

"So you did."

Dixie carried the smaller suitcase and the tote with her paints. Cole grabbed the other suitcase and the huge roll of untreated canvas. This diminished but didn't empty the pile in her suvvy.

The door to the carriage house was unlocked. Dixie pushed it open and stopped a foot inside.

Nothing had changed. From the pine paneling to

the white curtains to the simple furniture, everything looked just as it had eleven years ago.

Cole nudged her. "Sightsee later. This is heavy. Are you sure you don't have a body rolled up inside?"

"Of course not. The blood would make a mess of my canvas."

"Your weights, then? Move, Dixie."

She moved, stopping beside the battered leather couch. The last time she'd seen that couch, she'd been naked. "Isn't this the same Navajo blanket on the back of the couch?" A bit worn now, but the colors were as beautiful faded as they had been new. Bemused, she ran a hand over it.

"I remember how it looked wrapped around you."

Her hand remained on the blanket. Her gaze flew to Cole's—and the past crashed into the present, smashing itself all over her, making a mess of her mind and her heartbeat.

At that moment she wanted him. Wanted him badly.

Twenty-two fuzzy pounds thumped against her leg, nearly knocking her over and making a noise like a chain saw.

Cole's eyes widened. "What in the world—?"

"Meet Hulk." *Thank you, Hulk,* she told him silently, bending to pick him up. He sprawled, limp with pleasure, over her shoulder while she ran a hand over cowlicky gray fur. Hulk loved attention.

"As in The Incredible?" Cole looked dubious. "He *is* a cat, right?"

"That's the rumor."

"I'd better let my mother know about him."

"She's not allergic or something, is she? Mercedes said it was okay to bring him." She rubbed him under the chin the way he liked, and his motor revved loudly. "He always travels with me."

"I'm sure it will be fine. I don't think she was prepared, though. She hasn't stocked the grounds with antelope or gazelle for him to feed on." He eyed the cat. "Good thing there aren't any small children in the neighborhood."

"Very funny. Hulk's big, but he's a sweetie. He loves everyone, children included."

"For dessert?"

She huffed out a breath. "What do you have against my cat?"

"Tilly."

"There shouldn't be a problem. If he has to, Hulk will take to a tree, but he isn't easily intimidated."

"Tilly is. Though terrified describes her better."

Oh. She grimaced. "I'll try to keep him in." She detached Hulk and poured him onto the couch. He gave her a reproachful look and jumped down. Cat honor demanded that he not stay where he'd been put, even if he wanted to.

It took three more trips to finish unloading her suvvy. Dixie managed not to slide back into memory land, but she was very ready for Cole to leave by the time they brought in the last few items. Her emotions were a jumble. She needed a sit.

With typical contrariness, once he'd deposited

her bag of books Cole seemed ready to stay and chat. "Weird pillow," he said, nodding at the zafu she'd placed on the floor by an empty wall. "Gives me all kinds of kinky thoughts."

"It's for my sits." When he looked blank she added, "Meditation, Cole. You have heard of meditation?"

"Ah." He nodded. "Does that mean you aren't practicing witchcraft anymore?"

"It wasn't my path." She huffed out an impatient breath. "Look, do you still run all the time?"

"Two or three times a week."

"That's your mental-health break. I sit."

He burst out laughing. "No, no—" he said, holding up a hand. "Don't blow up at me. I just thought that I should have known you'd prefer sitting to running."

She couldn't help grinning. It *was* appropriate. "I can't see the appeal in sweating." Though it was hard to argue with the results. Cole was as lean and sculpted at thirty-five as he'd been at twenty-four.

At least, he seemed to be. A dress shirt and slacks don't make everything clear… *Don't go there,* she told her imagination.

He leaned against the wall, crossing his arms over his chest. "Going to offer me a cold drink now that I've flexed my muscles for you?"

"You didn't put on the tank shirt," she pointed out, setting her laptop on the table. "Besides, I haven't been to the store yet."

"Mother will have seen that the refrigerator and pantry are stocked with the basics." He cocked his head. "Nervous, Dixie?"

"Of course not." Oh, God would get her for that lie. "But I do need to get settled in. Shouldn't you be working?"

"I've been known to go for whole minutes at a time without my calculator these days. So why are you here?"

She blinked. "You're having a little trouble with your memory?"

"You're in a position to pick and choose your jobs. You picked Louret. I want to know why."

She made her shrug as casual as she could, considering the irritating way her heartbeat was behaving. "First, you're paying me a good deal of money. Second, Mercedes asked me to do it. Third…while ignoring your existence has been a pleasant habit, it's getting in the way of my friendship with your sister now that I'm back in California."

"So you're here because of me." He started toward her.

"Your ego is showing."

"Call it unfinished business, then."

He was standing too close, but damned if she was going to retreat. "That's part of it. A small part."

"Good." He leaned in even closer and kissed her.

Shock held her still for the first instant, long enough for the liquid roll of desire to hit. Instinct had her reacting in the next.

She shoved him. Hard.

He staggered back a step, tripped over Hulk and fell flat on his butt.

Dixie burst out laughing.

To her surprise, he chuckled, too. "The idea was for me to sweep you off your feet, not to get knocked off mine. Your demon cat—"

"You'd better not have hurt him." She looked around and saw Hulk sitting by the couch, busily smoothing his ruffled fur with his tongue. No damage there, obviously.

"That's right. Worry about your cat, not me."

"You're bigger than he is."

"Not by much." But he was grinning as he got to his feet.

She raised her eyebrows. "You have changed."

"I'm not twenty-four anymore." The smile lingered on his mouth, but his eyes held a different message. One that hit her harder than that so-brief kiss. "Understand this—what we had eleven years ago is a closed account. That doesn't keep us from opening a new one."

"I'm not interested." Her body might be, but her body wasn't in charge.

"I am. Tell me—do you still have that tattoo?"

"Go away, Cole."

"I'll be out of town for a couple days, but when I come back, I plan to find out about that tattoo." With that he turned and left, pulling the door closed behind him.

All sorts of emotions jostled around inside Dixie. She bit her lip. For a second she tasted him again, salt and coffee and the subtle blend that was pure Cole. Oddly, though, her ghosts were silent.

Maybe memories are like the moon, she thought. Reflected light is never as bright and strong as what you get direct from the source…and the source of her ghosts had just kissed her for the first time since she left him eleven years ago.

Shouldn't she be cautioning herself about all sorts of things?

But the interior tumult gradually settled into a smile, and it was filled with speculation, not nostalgia. She'd agreed to the job as a favor to Mercedes and because she did need to deal with some ghosts. But curiosity had played a part, too.

It looked as if the next two weeks would be anything but boring.

Early in the morning the following Monday, Dixie went strolling along the curving driveway that circled the front of the property, looking for a gray blob. Hulk had gotten out. He'd managed to do that at least once a day since she arrived.

Not that it mattered. Cole had left on a business trip the day after Dixie got here. He'd taken Tilly with him.

"Hey, Hulk," she called. Dawn had arrived, but the bank of storm clouds nearly hid the fact. The wind was blustery, promising rain, and the temperature was a cool forty-five degrees. "You know how you hate to get wet. Time to come in." No sign of him.

It was probably just as well Cole had taken off. The reminder of his priorities could only be good for her, even if, like a lot of things that are good for you, it tasted nasty going down. But dammit, when a man announces his intention of inspecting a woman's tattoo, he ought to stay around long enough for her to turn him down.

Funny how alike she and Cole were in some ways, she thought, crossing to the next row. Most people don't take their pets with them on business trips. Yet in other ways, they stood on opposite sides of a chasm.

Of course, it wouldn't be odd for Tilly to go with him if it wasn't really business that had taken him away.

No. She shook her head. Cole had faults—huge, heaping bunches of them. But unless he'd changed beyond all recognition, he played fair. No lies, no tricks. Besides, she couldn't picture his mother fibbing for him.

Dixie smiled. She liked Caroline Ashton Sheppard, even if the woman was the source of some of Cole's more irritating assumptions about the female half of the gender divide. Had Caroline been born a couple thousand miles to the east, she would have made a great Southern belle—gentle, soft-spoken, with an innate sense of style and a will of iron.

She liked Cole's stepfather, too. Lucas Sheppard was one of those salt-of-the-earth types who serve as a reminder to cynics like her that not all men are cads, little boys or idiots.

Another thing she and Cole had in common, she thought wryly. They both had father issues.

Of course, his went a lot deeper. Dixie's father hadn't meant to die and leave her, while Cole's father had abandoned him intentionally. Not that Cole had told Dixie about it, not Mr. I-Don't-Talk-About-Personal-Stuff. But Mercedes had. When Cole was eight, Spencer Ashton had walked out on his family to marry his secretary, somehow swindling his wife out of most of her inheritance. He'd never looked back.

There was no sign of Hulk. Dixie called again, but she didn't expect him to answer. Hulk would show up when he darned well pleased.

Ah, well. She'd felt duty bound to try. Shaking her head, she turned and headed back. Even in winter the vineyards were a pleasant place to stroll, with the aisles between the rows of vines green with a cover crop of legumes and barley. Russ had told her the plants would be tilled under in the spring, adding nitrogen to the soil.

Sure didn't seem like winter, though. The grass was green, for one thing. Most people grew cool-season grasses here, and that's what she'd grown up with…but she'd been away a long time. Long enough for it to seem both strange and strangely familiar to wander around outside in January without bundling up.

Which led to the subject of clothes. She had a winter wardrobe she'd not be able to…

Who was that? Dixie stopped, frowning. There

was a man standing in front of The Vines. Not one of the vineyard workers, she thought, though he was dressed casually, in jeans and a plain shirt. But she'd met all of the workers now, hadn't she?

Maybe not. She'd have remembered this one—a tall, rugged sort, he looked as if he'd just ridden in off the range. Though there was something vaguely familiar about him...intrigued, she headed his way.

"Hello," she said as she drew near. "You looking for someone?"

He turned. There was gray in his dark hair and interesting crinkles around his eyes—from squinting as he rode off into the sunset, she decided, amused by herself. "Not really. Just curious."

"The winery loves curious tourists," she assured him, "but not until ten o'clock, when the tasting room opens. This area is private property." She cocked her head. "You look familiar."

"I don't think we've met," he said politely. "Are you one of the owners? The, ah, Ashtons?"

"No, just a temporary employee and a friend. It's the head shape," she said, pleased to have figured it out. "And something about the set of the eyes. If I could line your skull up next to Cole's and Eli's, I'll bet the occipital surfaces and zygomatic arches would be identical."

He looked faintly alarmed. "I hope you don't plan to make the attempt. You're a doctor? Or an anthropologist?"

She laughed. "None of the above. An artist. You

wouldn't be some long-lost Ashton cousin, would you?"

He shook his head and studied her a moment longer, a faint smile on his mouth, something unreadable in his eyes. "I'd better be going, since this is private property. Nice speaking with you."

Cole had spent four frustrating days in Sacramento. Some of the frustration had been professional, but a fair portion arose from his inability to keep his mind where it belonged.

Dixie had left The Vines on Friday afternoon, planning to be gone all weekend. Which she was entitled to do, of course. But Cole kept wondering who she was spending the weekend with. A woman like Dixie was only alone if she wanted to be.

At two o'clock that morning, alone in his hotel room, he'd been fighting with memories and questioning his sanity. Why in the world would he consider getting involved with her again?

He was attracted, yes. What man wouldn't be, especially if he knew just how hot it could be between them? But he was old enough to know that fire burns, and long past the point where he could be led around by his gonads.

He didn't need the heartache or the hassle, he'd finally decided, and had at last dropped off to sleep.

So it was annoying to learn, as he pulled into the parking lot at the winery, that he was looking forward to seeing her again. He grabbed his briefcase, opened the Jeep's door and slid out.

Eli was waiting for him. "How'd it go?"

"Lots of talk, not much action." He opened the back door and Tilly jumped down, politely sniffed Eli's hand, then wandered away to check out the shrubbery in front of the tasting room.

"Everyone agrees that we need better coordination between the various growers' associations," Cole said, opening his briefcase and removing a stack of papers. "Especially when it comes to lobbying in Sacramento. No one wants to actually do the work of setting up a coordinating group."

"I thought Joe Bradley was keen on running things."

"I'm not letting Joe turn this into one of his dog-and-pony shows. He starts out big, loses interest and then things fizzle."

Eli sighed. "I suppose that means you agreed to run things."

"Nope." Cole was still mildly astonished at himself. Somewhere along the line, though, doing it all—and proving he could do it better—had stopped being fun. "I've got enough on my plate already."

"I know that. I didn't think you did."

"Here," Cole said, handing Eli the papers. "A copy of the minutes. There are a few things of interest in there."

Eli scowled. "Summarize it for me."

Cole grinned. Eli's hatred of paperwork was a chain he loved to yank. "Can't. I've got enough on my plate."

"I'm going to break that damn plate over your

head," Eli informed him without heat. "This new leaf of yours doesn't have anything to do with that old girlfriend of yours who's following me around, does it?"

"Dixie is following you around?" He made that sound so casual he almost believed himself.

"Everywhere I turn, there she is with that blasted camera. Says she wants lots of candid shots before she starts painting." Eli grimaced. "Why the hell didn't you and Mercedes tell me this promotional campaign was going to use my face?"

"It's more fun to surprise you." Cole started for the door.

"Well, I don't like it." Eli fell into step beside him. "Not that I have any problem with Dixie's company."

"Who would?" She'd undoubtedly been flirting with Eli, Cole thought. For Dixie, flirting came as naturally as breathing.

"She's fun to have around, not to mention being eye candy from top to toe. I just wish she'd ditch the camera." Eli stopped, facing Cole so that he had to stop, too. "So…you have any claim there?"

Cole's eyebrows snapped down. "With Dixie?"

"I think that's who we're talking about, yeah. I know the two of you had something going years ago, but you don't seem to be picking up where you left off."

"I've been in Sacramento," Cole snapped. Just because he'd decided to step back didn't mean he wanted to watch his brother move in.

"And I've been here, and I've been looking. Thought I'd better let you know before I made a move."

"You can't find a woman of your own?" Cole demanded, furious. "You want my hand-me-downs?"

Eli infuriated him by chuckling. "I'd like to be there when Dixie hears you refer to her as hand-me-downs."

He wasn't entirely crazy. "Bad choice of words," he admitted. "But you'd still better keep your greedy hands to yourself."

"We'll see. If you don't—"

Tilly rounded the corner of the building at a dead run, hotly pursued by a huge gray cat. The dog skidded to a halt behind Cole's legs, trembling. And Dixie rounded the corner at a run—face flushed, long hair flying, long legs bare beneath ragged cutoffs.

She jerked to a stop several feet away. So did Hulk, but Cole wasn't looking at the cat.

He was older and wiser now…but flexibility was an aspect of maturity, right? He could change his mind.

Three

Cole's mouth kicked up in a grin. "I don't think I've ever seen you move that fast before."

"I was trying to rescue your stupid dog." She was out of breath and disheveled, her chest heaving beneath a skimpy T-shirt that read, Well-Behaved Women Seldom Make History.

Tilly was calmer now that she'd found backup, though she still huddled behind Cole. He ran a hand over the top of her head soothingly and tried to sound severe. "You're supposed to keep your demon cat inside."

"Guess what? He got out."

"Wouldn't matter," Eli said, "if Cole's dog weren't so pathetic." He looked at Tilly, crouched behind Cole. "I know the cat is big, but you still out-weigh him by fifty pounds."

"Like that matters." Cole shook his head. "As far as Tilly's concerned, everything in the world is bigger and meaner than she is."

Dixie sauntered closer, as casually graceful as her cat and a lot more interesting to watch. "She may be right about meaner. I've seen earthworms with more backbone."

"Earthworms are invertebrates."

"You get my point."

Eli had been noticing Dixie's legs. In all conscience, Cole couldn't blame him. "Aren't you cold?" Eli asked, concerned. "This isn't exactly shorts weather."

Cole could have warned him not to suggest that Dixie didn't know what she was doing at all times. He wouldn't have, of course, but he could have.

Dixie eyebrows flew up. "It's shorts weather to me. I've gotten used to a more rugged climate."

"Rugged." Cole nodded. "Yeah, that's the first word I think of when I think of you. I like the T-shirt."

"I noticed that you'd become a slow reader."

Since the letters were stretched across a pair of lovely breasts, he just grinned.

While they were talking, Hulk was infiltrating. Nonchalant as only a cat can be, he'd wandered closer. Tilly kept retreating until she was behind Eli. Hulk, triumphant, stropped himself against Cole's leg, purring.

"Yeah, I can see how innocent you are," Cole said, bending to pick the cat up. He promptly went limp, purring manically. Automatically Cole stroked him.

Dixie smirked. "He likes to be rubbed behind the ears."

"That's a dog thing."

"Tell him, not me."

"Okay, I get it." Eli nodded. "See you two later."

Cole glanced at him. "What are you talking about?"

"Going back to work. You remember about work? It's something some of us like to do at this hour on a weekday."

"Good idea." Cole looked back at Dixie. "Take Tilly with you."

"Forget it. You deserve a few handicaps. Nice to see you without that camera, Dixie," he said, then headed off.

Dixie watched Eli leave, looking vexed. "I like your brother."

"So do I, at times." Especially when Eli had the good sense to go away. "Why does that bug you?"

She huffed out a breath. "I wasn't paying attention, I guess. Of course, he's very closed up, even worse than you. Hard to read. But I was *not* trying to play the two of you off each other."

"I didn't think you were. You can't help flirting— that's like breathing for you. A process I enjoyed watching, by the way, while reading your T-shirt, but never mind that for now. You don't play men off each other. That would be calculated, and there's nothing calculating about you."

"That came perilously close to a compliment on something other than my breasts. Backhanded, but averaging more positive than negative."

"Don't let it go to your head. Here." He held out twenty pounds of limp feline. "Take your monster. Tilly's having a breakdown trying to figure out how to hide behind me when I'm holding her enemy."

She draped the beast over her shoulder and started at an easy pace for the carriage house. Cole fell into step beside her.

Dixie slid him a sideways glance. "You think Tilly has some kind of canine PTSD?"

"I'm putting it down to poor parenting. Her former owner must have mistreated her."

"She was previously owned by a cat?"

His lips twitched. "I'd say her fears generalized."

She smiled, but fleetingly, and didn't respond. For a few minutes they walked together in silence, with Tilly on Cole's other side.

Funny, he thought. He'd once found it irksome to walk with Dixie. They'd matched up great in bed, but he hadn't liked matching his steps to hers. She strolled. He wanted to get where he was going as efficiently as possible.

She'd said she didn't see the appeal in sweating. He didn't see the point in taking twenty minutes to get somewhere if you could do it in ten. But it was okay to slow down occasionally, he decided. It gave him a chance to notice the subtle scent she wore…slightly spicy, more herbal than floral, hard to pin down.

Like her. "What did you think of New York?"

"I loved it," she said promptly. "Even during my homesick period, when I was in this horrible little apartment and didn't know anyone, I loved it. There's so much to see and do, and the energy is incredible."

"You liked that? I never could picture you there, part of that lickety-split New York energy."

"You always saw me as a lazy flake," she said philosophically.

"No, I didn't." When she looked at him, all skepticism, he conceded, "An artistic flake, maybe. Not the same thing. You saw me as a dull business grunt."

"Never dull," she murmured. "Driven."

"A word that conjures the echoes of a few of our better arguments."

"Your definition for better being…?" She shook her head. "Never mind. You never wanted to move away, try a new place, did you?"

"My goals, my family, my life—they were all here. They still are. Why did you leave?" As soon as the words were out, Cole wanted to call them back. They'd come out too abruptly, sounding too much like *why did you leave me?*

He knew why. Eventually he'd understood and even agreed with her. Understanding wasn't the same as forgiving.

Either she didn't hear the unspoken question or she didn't want to go there, either. "Itchy feet," she said lightly. "You know what they say about New York—'if you can make it there, you'll make it anywhere.' I wanted to see if I could make it."

"You succeeded." They'd reached the carriage house. He opened the door and held it.

"Women and monsters first."

"Just the monster. I've got to get back to work. What?" she demanded. "What's so funny?"

"You're in a hurry to get back to work and I'm not."

"Okay, that is weird. Be ready to close the door fast." She dumped Hulk onto the floor, stepped back and Cole closed the door—fast, as ordered, with Hulk on the other side and complaining about it. "The deadline for the first painting is pretty tight, and I haven't got it settled yet in my mind. Eli's the subject, but I don't have the right angle on him."

"You pay attention to deadlines?" he asked politely.

"Very funny. I'm not that bad."

"If you tell me you're always on time now, I'll have to ask for ID. Or maybe consult an exorcist."

She grinned. "At least you admit it's demonic to be compulsively punctual."

Her grin was too familiar. It tugged at places inside him that he preferred to keep private. Cole put a hand on the door, keeping her where she was, and leaned in closer. "These are new," he observed, touching his thumb to the corner of one eye, where a faint smile line showed.

She jerked her head away. "You used to be better with compliments. Back off, Cole."

"I'm not going to kiss you. Not right this minute, anyway." He'd forgotten the flecks of gold in her eyes, and how they turned plain brown to a rich caramel.

Her eyebrows lifted in haughty offense over those caramel eyes—but her tongue darted out to moisten her lip. "I see. You suddenly felt weak and couldn't stand up on your own."

"You're nervous. I like that."

"You're obnoxious. I don't like that."

He chuckled and straightened. "How long will you be here at The Vines, Dixie?"

She regarded him suspiciously. "Why?"

"I need to know what my deadline is."

"If I ask why again, and you tell me, am I going to be mad?"

"Probably. No, almost certainly."

"Then we'll skip the questions and go straight to the answers. I'll be here for about two weeks, and I'm not going to bed with you. And now I really need to get back to work." She started back toward the winery.

She was moving faster than usual, he noted. "You're passing up the chance to throw a great temper fit."

"I don't throw fits. Or anything else."

"Lost that artistic temperament, have you? I seem to recall a plate that came sailing my way once. I could have sworn you were mad."

Her lips thinned—but it looked more like an effort to hold back a smile than real temper. "Tell me, Cole. Is this your version of dipping my pigtails in the ink to get my attention? Or are you really spoiling for a fight?"

"Want to watch me turn somersaults? Or I could do chin-ups. They're more macho."

The smile won. She paused. "Push-ups. There's something so manly about push-ups."

He promptly dropped to the ground and began doing push-ups.

She laughed in delight and sat smack-dab on the cold ground to watch, propping her chin on her hand. "Ooh, look at those muscles. You're so strong."

"Don't forget—" he managed one more "—manly. Strong and manly." He stopped before he could embarrass himself, rolling onto his back and sitting up. Maybe he needed to add more upper-body training to his routine. His arms felt rubbery. "That was harder than it looked," he assured her.

"I can't believe you did it—and in dress slacks, yet."

He was surprised, too. "It worked. You quit running away."

"I wasn't running." She drew up her legs and hugged her knees.

"Okay, walking away." He wished she'd stretch her legs out again. Dixie had great legs—firm calves, narrow ankles. He wanted to run a hand up one of them.

"Quit staring at my legs."

"I'm checking for goose bumps. What did you

do—get up and say, 'I'm in California, therefore I must wear shorts?'"

Her mouth twitched reluctantly. "Something like that. It's *almost* warm enough for them."

He leaned back on one hand. "Why the evasive tactics, Dixie? Do you really want me to go away?"

She shrugged, not looking at him. "When I decided to take this job, I wasn't expecting you to put on a full-court press. I tried not to have any expectations at all, but in the back of my mind I guess I thought you'd be in your chill zone with me."

Cole didn't want to hear about how cold she thought he was. "I keep telling you I'm not twenty-four anymore."

"It's damned disconcerting, too." She plucked a blade of grass and ran it up her bare leg. "Like going home after years away and seeing old buildings gone, new ones put up. You turn a corner expecting to see the Wilson's frame house, but they're long gone and the new people have stuccoed the exterior and cut down the big oak tree. So much is the same, but I keep tripping over the differences."

"You've been home for visits, though, haven't you?"

She slid him an amused look. "I was speaking metaphorically."

"I got that. I just wondered if you'd avoided California altogether." And why she'd returned.

"I come back once or twice a year to see Mom and Aunt Jody." She pulled up some more grass and let it sift through her fingers. "Mom's getting married again."

"Yeah?" He tried to sound as if this was a good idea.

Her wry look told him he hadn't pulled it off. "This time it might work. Mike's a good guy."

Cole could barely call up an image of Helen McCord Lynchfield. He'd only met Dixie's mother once…and that seemed odd, now that he thought about it.

Of course, their affair had only lasted a little over three months, though they'd known each other off and on ever since Mercedes went off to college. Merry and Dixie had been roommates, and Dixie had come home with her several times during breaks. There'd been trouble at home. The man who'd been her stepfather at the time had been a grade-A bastard.

Dixie's mother had finally left the bastard a month before Dixie graduated. And a month after that, the Valley had sweated under a record-setting heat wave. Cole and Dixie had claimed responsibility for that.

"I imagine your mom is glad to have you nearby. And your aunt, too. She's still in L.A.?" In some ways, Dixie was closer to her mother's sister, an award-winning reporter, than to her mother. While Cole could understand why, it had always made him wary. Jody Belleview was a funny, fiercely independent woman with a finely developed scorn for marriage.

"Aunt Jody's not in L.A. anymore."

Something in Dixie's voice caught his attention.

She was looking down at a small patch of ground she'd absentmindedly denuded of grass. "What is it, Dix?"

"She's the reason I moved back here. Mom couldn't take care of her by herself anymore."

A quick squeeze of hurt for her had him covering her hand with his. "That sounds bad."

"Pretty bad, yeah. She has Alzheimer's."

Stunned, Cole just sat there. He'd met Dixie's aunt just once, at the same time he met her mother. But Jody Belleview was the kind of woman who left an impression. He remembered her laugh and her quick, restless intelligence. "I can't imagine…isn't she younger than your mother? Only fifty or so?"

"Fifty-four. I'm still in denial. Which is not as easy to do on this coast as it was while I was across the country." She gave him a brittle smile, then gathered herself and rose to her feet.

He stood, too. "Dixie—"

She shook her head. "I'm sorry. I can't talk about it."

When she walked away she was moving fast, not strolling, her back straight and stiff. And Cole just stood there and let her go, feeling as if the earth had shifted under him.

She couldn't talk about it? That didn't sound like Dixie. Maybe she meant she couldn't talk about it with him…but that wasn't what she'd said. It wasn't what he'd felt radiating from her with the kind of buried intensity he knew only too well.

He was the one who stuffed things into compartments, banged the lid shut and sat on it to keep them there. Dixie had always possessed a terrifying honesty, with herself as well as others. She lifted lids and peeked inside. She didn't turn away from painful truths.

At least, that's how he remembered her.

Cole stood there a few moments longer, frowning at the path she'd vanished down. Then he went looking for his sister.

Four

At ten o'clock that night, Dixie stood on a drop cloth in the center of her temporary living room, slashing color across a canvas. The light was lousy for painting, but it didn't matter. She wasn't really painting. She was venting. No one but her would ever see this.

Red roiled with brown in a muddy whirlpool at the lower right, while a mountain of black and gray reared over a pale green center like a granite wave about to crash. It was lousy art, she thought, stepping back to look it over. But damn satisfying.

The knock on her door brought a frown to her face. On the couch, Hulk lifted his head, lazily contemplating the possibility of company. To Hulk, company meant someone who could be cozened into rubbing his jaw or chin. To Dixie, it meant conversation.

She didn't want to talk. She considered not answering, but it probably wouldn't work. Scowling, she snapped, "Just a minute," then poked her brush into the wire loop that held it in the cleaner. She grabbed a rag and wiped some of the paint from her fingers as she headed to the door.

Cole stood on her stoop with a frown to match her own—and a small leather tote in one hand, like an overnight case.

She eyed that tote, eyebrows raised. "Not exactly subtle, Cole."

"It doesn't hold my shaving gear. No full-court press tonight. No moves, no passes, no fouls. May I come in?"

She studied his face. It didn't tell her much. "Why not?" she said at last, and stepped back.

"I did some research," he said as he entered. "Nothing you haven't already read, probably, but…" Words and feet both drifted to a stop as he saw her easel in the center of the room. And what sat on the easel.

In spite of her mood, his expression tickled her.

"Interesting," he said after a moment in a careful voice. "I thought you didn't do that kind of abstract art."

She chuckled. "That isn't art, it's therapy. My version of smashing crockery."

"That would be why it looks like crap, then."

"Probably. I'll scrape the canvas and reprime it

later." She cocked her head to one side. "You aren't here to inspect my visual therapy."

"No, I..." Hulk had abandoned the couch and was rubbing against Cole's leg, making like a chain saw. Cole bent and rubbed behind his ears. "Hello, monster."

Dixie ambled over to retrieve her brush, which ·ceded to be washed. She'd made the canvas about .s ugly as it needed to be. Might as well shut down for the night and find out what Cole was up to.

In the tiny kitchen, she turned on the tap and worked soap into the soft bristles. "Hulk appreciates company, no matter what the hour. I'm not in the mood."

"Tough." He'd set the mysterious tote on the coffee table. "You probably know all this," he said gruffly, taking out a fat folder, "but I wasn't sure how far your denial extended, so I thought I'd pass it on."

She put down her brush and returned to the living area, curious. He handed her the folder. Inside, she found pages and pages of information—about Alzheimer's. Organized into sections, with neatly printed tab tops dividing them: Stages...Treatments...Theories...Caretaker Support...

"That's all from reputable sites," he told her. "There's a lot of information out there, but not all of it is reliable."

"This must have taken hours," she murmured, paging through the printouts.

"I wanted to know about your aunt's condition, and you weren't talking. Which brings us to another question."

She looked up. "Us?"

"All right, me. It brings me to another question." He moved restlessly, paused to frown at her visual therapy, then looked back at her. "Why aren't you talking about it?" he demanded.

"Just because I didn't talk to you—"

"You haven't unloaded on Mercedes, either."

"I told her about Aunt Jody," she protested.

"Yeah, and that's all. You haven't…you know." He waved vaguely. "Talked about your feelings."

"Ah…" Deep inside, a laugh was trying to climb out. "Let me get this straight. *You* are nagging *me* to talk about my feelings?"

"Bottling everything up—that's my deal. I'm used to that. Comfortable with it. You aren't." He sat on her couch without waiting for an invitation and began pulling more things out of his tote and putting them on the pine coffee table.

A bottle of wine. Two glasses. A box of chocolates. Nail polish. Peppermint-scented foot lotion. Cotton balls. Polish remover.

She sank down on the other end of the couch. The laugh was getting closer to the top. She waved weakly at the objects on the coffee table. "Cole? You want to clue me in here?"

"Just call me Sheila. I'm a stand-in."

"For?" A smile started.

"This is one of those female parties. The kind where you women get together to do each other's hair or nails and end up telling each other the damnedest things." He shook his head, marveling.

Oh. *Oh.* He was giving her every signal he could, even playing surrogate female, to tell her he was here as a friend, and nothing more. Because he was worried about her. Dixie's eye's filled. She stood, took two quick steps, bent and kissed him on the cheek. "This is about the sweetest thing…thank you."

"You're not going to cry, are you?"

She laughed. And if it came out a bit watery, tough. "I'm not making any promises. Are you going to paint your nails or mine?"

"I'm going to drink the wine." He inserted the bottle opener and twisted. He had strong hands, and they made quick work of the cork. "But you're welcome to join me."

"Does cabernet sauvignon go with chocolate?" She sat down and opened the box of candy. "Mmm. Dark chocolate at that."

"Mercedes seemed to think chocolate was essential."

She slid him a look. "You talked about this with Merry?"

"Yeah." He poured wine into one of the glasses, and its heady perfume drifted her way. "For some reason she thinks you're fine."

"Maybe because I am." She selected one she thought might have caramel. She loved caramel.

"Glad to hear it. So what do you talk about at these female shindigs?"

"Pretty much anything—men, work, hair, men, family, movies, men, books, politics…did I mention men?"

"The rat bastards," he said promptly, handing her a glass of wine. Hulk jumped up beside him and pointed out that no one was petting him by bumping his head against Cole's arm. Wine sloshed in the glass without spilling. Absently he began scratching the side of Hulk's face. "They never call."

Dixie shook her head sadly. "Or remember your birthday."

"And if they do, they forget the card. Would it kill them to spend some time picking out a card?"

"So true. And they only want one thing."

"Damn straight. Uh-oh. Sorry—I slid out of character there for a moment."

"Watch it." She took a sip, trying to keep a straight face. "Hey, this is good."

"Ninety-eight was one of our better years." He swirled the wine in his glass to release the scent, held it up and inhaled, his eyes half-closed. For a moment she glimpsed the closet sybarite in the pure, sensual pleasure on his face. Cole was a deeply sensual man. He mostly didn't let it show. "It's aging well," he observed, and took a sip.

"So what were you doing in ninety-eight?" She leaned back and nibbled at her chocolate. She liked to eat them slowly, let the taste melt into her tongue. "Note that I don't ask *who* you were doing."

"I'd get in trouble if I put it that way." He continued to send Hulk into a stupor of delight with those elegant fingers.

Quit staring at his hands, she told herself.

"Women can say things to each other that men can't get away with."

"So you talk about sex at these things?"

"Sure. It's a subheading under men. For most of us," she added. "I had a couple of lesbian friends in New York—my downstairs neighbors. We mostly did not talk about sex, out of consideration for my comfort level."

He chuckled. "My comfort level, on the other hand—"

"Don't go there, Sheila." She reconsidered. "On the other hand, I've always wondered why men get excited by—"

"You were right the first time," he said. There was a spark of amusement—and something else, something warmer—in his eyes as he took another sip of wine. "We'd better skip the sex talk."

She met his eyes as she took another sip, letting the wine sit on her tongue for a moment to develop the secondary flavors the way he'd taught her.

Not a good idea, enjoying her own sensual side while looking at Cole. "A hint of blackberry," she said hastily, looking away. "See how well I know the lingo? Should be nice with chocolate." She took another nibble of that. "Want to argue about politics?"

"Not the effect I'm going for tonight."

"You probably voted for the governor," she said darkly. "All right, all right—I won't get into that. So we're left discussing work or hair. I vote for hair." She tilted her head. "Who does yours?"

"Carmen at The Mane Place. She has magic fingers. I like your hair." The warmth in his voice did not belong to anyone named Sheila, unless Sheila had been of the same persuasion as Dixie's New York neighbors. "You left out a couple choices. Movies, books…family."

She took a healthy swallow of wine. "Read any good books lately?"

"No. How's your mom?"

She huffed out an impatient sigh. "Your male side is showing, Sheila."

So he asked again, but in an absurd falsetto, "How's your mom?"

Dixie nearly choked, trying not to laugh, and gave up. "The same as ever, pretty much. Only happier."

"Because of this man she's going to marry?"

Dixie nodded, sipped, and a smile slipped out. "She always used to try so hard with whatever man she thought was going to fix everything for her. With Mike, she's relaxed. She isn't desperate to make him happy, or trying too hard to be happy herself. She just feels good with him, and it shows. Not that she doesn't hurt because of what's happening to Jody, but she's… I don't know. Somehow she's okay about it."

"You aren't okay about it."

She frowned, not answering. He didn't say anything, either. Just sat there and sipped and petted Hulk, watching her.

"All right." She set her glass down with a snap. "All right! You want to hear about my feelings? I'm mad. Pissed as hell."

"You would be, of course."

She shoved to her feet and started to pace. "It's so horrible and so unfair. She still knows who we are. She isn't so far gone that she's lost that, but she will. She's already lost so many pieces of herself, and it hurts me. This shouldn't be about me, but every time I see her…the bewildered look on her face… My mother's dealing with this so much better than I am."

"She's been here, watching it happen. She's had time to adjust."

"And I've been on the other side of the continent, letting her deal with everything. You know what makes me crazy?" She stopped, shook her head. "Never mind. It's stupid."

"I have no problem with you being stupid."

"You're in danger of slipping out of supportive-friend mode," she warned him.

"Afraid you'll shock me?"

"No." She took two steps, stopped and threaded the fingers of both hands through her hair. "It's all this praise I keep getting. It makes me nuts."

"Yeah, I hate it when people praise me."

"Very funny. You know how often I hear some version of how strong I am?" she demanded. "Or that I'm such a great daughter and niece for moving back here. God. Aunt Jody was diagnosed two years ago. Two years. And I'm just now showing up."

"I guess you haven't done anything to help these past two years."

"I sent money. Big deal. I gave up a couple of vacations, flew out for more of the holidays. Then I'd go home and throw myself into work so I wouldn't have to think about Jody."

He shook his head. "Now that I can't understand. Throwing yourself into work to avoid dealing with something? You mystify me."

A reluctant smile touched her mouth. "You hinting that you have some experience in those lines?"

"I might." He stood, ignoring Hulk's protest at being disarranged. Crossing to her, he rested his hands on her shoulders. "What is it you think you should be doing differently, Dixie? Hurting less? Fixing things so your aunt doesn't hurt?"

"Don't forget the part about keeping my mother from hurting, too." The shape of his hands woke a visceral memory, a wordless surge of feeling that tangled past and present. She swallowed. "I said it was stupid."

"According to you, feelings are never stupid. They just are. It's what we do about them that matters."

"I could have sworn you never listened to my preaching."

Cole smiled that half up, half down smile without answering.

Dixie felt the impact low in her belly. Her heartbeat picked up as the present turned compelling, wiping out the whispers from the past. Desire bit, sharp and sweet. Her lips parted.

His gaze dipped there, lingered. His hands tightened on her shoulders, and the look on his face was unmistakable. He was going to kiss her…and she wanted that, wanted the taste and heat of him.

He dropped his hands and stepped back, his smile lost.

The disappointment was as disorienting as his sudden retreat. She put a hand on her stomach as if she could ease the sense of loss that way and tried to sound amused. "What was that? An attack of nobility, or common sense?"

He snorted. "You think I know?" He turned away, heading for the door. "This was a dumb idea. Enjoy the wine and chocolate and carry on with the nail painting. I'm leaving before I forget Sheila entirely."

"Cole."

He paused but didn't look at her.

"I was the one who switched the dial to another channel, not you. You…what you did helped."

He glanced back at her, conflicted emotions chasing over his face before he got it smoothed out. "Does this mean I'm invited to your next sleepover?"

"Not likely," she said dryly.

"Good. Because the next time I visit you at night, I won't be planning to sleep."

After the door closed behind him, Hulk came over, voicing his protest at being abandoned. "Don't come complaining to me," Dixie muttered, contradicting her words by picking him up and rubbing behind his ears. "At least you got stroked for a while. I didn't."

Which she ought to feel a lot better about, dammit.

Five

Louret's cellars had been a disappointment to Dixie when Cole first showed them to her. She'd hoped for earthen-floored caves or something appropriately dungeonlike. Instead, the barrels and bottles were aged in perfectly ordinary underground rooms with high-tech climate control and lousy lighting.

Lousy from her perspective, that is. To a wine-maker, the dim lighting was necessary, as was strict control of temperature and humidity. But her imaginings would have made such a cool setting for Eli's painting…*well,* she thought, studying the barrels from her vantage point on the cement floor, *you work with what you've got.*

The barrels themselves were interesting. She'd

use lots of browns in the painting, she decided. Earth tones would suit Eli and suggest Louret's old-fashioned, hands-on approach while evoking the earth the grapes sprang from.

And gold for Caroline's painting, she decided, staring dreamily into space. Hints of brown to tie it to the earth and Eli's painting, touches of blue for the sky, and lots of gold—pale, glowing gold, like the sunlight that joins earth and sky.

Oh, yes. She'd use Eli and the barrels for the earth the vines were grown in, Caroline for the golden sunshine that made the grapes rich. For the end product, the wine itself…maybe a group picture? The family gathered around the dinner table, talking and interacting, their wineglasses catching the glow of sunset.

Set it outside then? And what about—

"Sorry I'm late," Eli's deep voice said from behind her.

"That's okay," she said, picking up her sketch pad and rising. "I don't think I'll draw you here, after all."

Uncertainty, she'd noticed, looked a lot like a scowl when it settled on Eli's face. "You aren't going to paint me with the barrels?"

"No, I'm definitely putting you against the barrels. But I've got photos for that. Today I need to draw you. Outside, I think. I need a peek at your bones. Strong light and shadows will help me get that." She gave him a smile as she passed, heading for the stairs.

After a moment she heard him following her up.

"You want to draw me outside, but you're not painting me outside."

"I use the photos for technical accuracy. Drawing helps me learn you. I don't know a subject until I've sketched him or her."

Eli looked pained. "I don't see why you need to use my face at all, but you don't have to, uh, know me to paint it."

She glanced over her shoulder as she reached the top of the stairs, mischief in her voice. "Oh, but I want more than your face for the painting. I want a bit of your soul."

He muttered something it was probably just as well she didn't catch. She was grinning as they stepped out the side door. "This will do." The light was good, strong and slanting. She got a charcoal pencil from her fanny pack and opened her sketch pad.

Eli squinted at the sunshine, looking profoundly uncomfortable. Better get him talking so he'd forget what she was up to. "Tell me about oaking," she said, her charcoal flying over the page. "I gather it's somewhat controversial?"

"More a matter of taste. Most people like some degree of oak. Heavy oaking can mask the subtleties of a really good red, but that's poor winemaking."

"What about whites? You're aging your new chardonnay in oak barrels." Needs to be heavier around the jaw, she decided, and darkened that line. "Is that standard?"

He shrugged. "Some use steel vats. We won't."

She had the definite impression he didn't think much of the winemakers who used steel. "Was that your decision or your mother's? With the new wine being named for her, I'd guess she had some input."

"Mostly mine. Mom likes the vanilla notes from oaking, though, so it was fine with her."

She flipped to a new page, shifted to get a different angle, and started another sketch. "And whose idea was the new chardonnay?"

"Cole's." He looked directly at her. "I thought you knew that."

"Okay, so I'm fishing." She frowned at the sketch. Something was off. The zygomatic arches? No, something about the way they related to his forehead. Dixie studied his brow line intently. "You missed your cue. You're supposed to discreetly fill me in on him without my having to ask."

He chuckled. It was an unexpected sound, coming from a man who tended toward angry or dour. "It's damned disconcerting to have you stare at me that way when you're talking about my brother. What did you want to know?"

She looked at him reproachfully and repeated, "*Without* my having to ask."

"Well, he's not seeing anyone right now, and he thinks you're hot."

"Mmm." Damn. It was his left eye—she'd set it too close to the bridge of the nose. Try again. She flipped to a new page. "I'm trying to come up with a modest way of saying, 'I know.'"

Again the low chuckle. "I think so, too. When I asked him if he'd staked a claim already—"

"You didn't."

"Of course I did. You two were involved before. I needed to know if he was interested. Funny thing is, he didn't seem to know, himself. I guess he's made up his mind now."

"I guess so." He seemed pretty sure that he wanted to get her into bed, anyway. "He claims he's mellowed."

"Mellow? Cole?" There was a note of humor in his voice, but it was fleeting. "Not the word I'd choose. He's got more control than I do, but there's a lot of intensity beneath that control."

"Good way to put it. He's still pretty wrapped up in the business, I guess." Her hand and eyes were working automatically now, which was just as well. Her mind wasn't on the sketch.

"He doesn't put in the sixty and eighty hour weeks he used to. That's why you left him, isn't it?"

Surprised, she looked at him—at Eli, that is, not at Eli's bones. Their eyes met. "That was a big part of it."

"Louret is always going to be important to him, and he's always going to like winning. You won't get a lap cat with Cole."

Annoyed, she sketched two tiny horns at the top of Eli's head. "I don't want a lap cat. I don't want to come last, either. There's bound to be something in between."

"It messed him up when you left."

"From my perspective, he was already messed up. So was I," she said, closing the sketch pad. "That was the problem."

Eli nodded. "That's valid. But this time...just be careful with him, okay? Don't promise more than you mean to follow through on."

"Are you asking my intentions?"

"I guess I am."

She smiled suddenly, took two quick steps and went up on tiptoes to kiss his cheek. "That's sweet. I don't have any idea what my intentions are yet, and when I do I'll let Cole know, not you. But it's sweet that you wanted to ask."

His ears turned red. "If you're finished with me, I've got stuff to do."

"I'm sure you do," she said, enjoying his embarrassment more than she should have. "I hope I'll be able to bring out your inner softie in the painting."

Now he was positively alarmed. "My what?"

She laughed and patted his arm. "Don't worry. Your portrait will be very manly."

Once Eli made his escape, though, her amusement evaporated. She was frowning as she headed for the carriage house so she could work on the composition for Eli's portrait.

It was only natural for Cole's brother to worry about him, she supposed. Only natural that he'd see her as the one at fault for having left Cole eleven years ago. But it left her feeling flat and a little lonely. There was no one worrying about her that way, no one warning her of potential heartbreak if she got involved with a man who'd hurt her before.

Not that she'd listen, she supposed wryly as she opened the door to her temporary home. But it might be nice to have someone worry, just this once.

"You used charcoal when you sketched Eli," Caroline observed.

"Mmm-hmm." Dixie's gaze flew back and forth between the woman in front of her and her sketch pad. Her pencil moved swiftly. They were in what Dixie thought of as the covered porch, though the family called it the lanai. It was open on the north side, which made the light good.

"I wondered why you're doing my sketch in pencil."

"I don't know." There was something about the flesh over the right cheek that wasn't right…Dixie smudged the shadow beneath the cheek with her finger to soften it, looked at Caroline again, then used the side of her pencil to pull the shadow back toward the ear.

Better. "I'll use the photos I took for technical precision," she explained. "The sketches are to learn you. When I get your shapes down with my hands, I know them, see? I wanted charcoal to learn Eli. I wanted pencil for you."

Caroline smiled. "My shape's rounder than it used to be. I suppose you have to show my double chin?"

"You don't have a double chin." Dixie spoke absently as she adjusted the brow line, which defined the eyes. "The jaw has softened with age, but… whoops. Forgot tact."

The older woman laughed. "Tell me something. Since you won't cater to my vanity in one way… you're sure it's okay if I talk?"

"Absolutely." Dixie turned to a new page, moved slightly to the left and began a gesture drawing from the new angle in a series of quick sweeps of her pencil.

"I've sometimes wondered if anything of me showed up in my boys. The girls, yes. I see something of myself in them. But Cole and Eli…"

Dixie heard another question in the way Caroline's voice trailed into silence. How much did her sons resemble the man who'd fathered and deserted them?

"The girls do take after you more than Eli and Cole do," she said casually, as if she hadn't noticed the unspoken part of the question. In Jillian's case the resemblance was more a matter of manner than genetics, but Dixie could be tactful when it mattered. "But Eli has your nose and your ears."

"And Cole?"

Cole…whom Mercedes said most resembled their father. "He has your hands. Great hands," she added, crouching for another angle. "I plan to use them."

When Caroline chuckled it took Dixie a moment to realize why. Then she flushed. "Ah…in the painting. I'm going to use your hands in the painting. Not

Cole's hands. I'm not planning to use them for, ah…"

Caroline smiled. "How delightful. I didn't think anything flustered you. You're a rather formidable young woman."

"Me?" Dixie was astonished. Caroline was the one with the inbred class and composure, the soft voice and gentle ways Cole had once thrown up at Dixie as the feminine ideal.

"But of course. Look at all you've accomplished at such a young age. Though I suppose you don't think of yourself as terribly youthful." Her smile turned amused. "The young never do. I hope I didn't insult you, dear. It's just that you're so very competent and confident. I wasn't, not at your age."

And yet what Dixie's pencil had captured was a calm, determined woman. She turned back to the finished sketch, then reversed her pad to show Caroline. "Here's what I see—strength, kindness, grace."

"Oh, my," Caroline said softly, taking the pad. "You've made it difficult for me to pry the way I'd intended. May I have this?"

"Of course." Dixie accepted the return of her sketch pad with a silent, fervent wish that Caroline would continue to find it difficult to pry.

"I don't know what you charge, but—"

"You'll insult me if you offer to pay. The paintings are business. This isn't."

"Then I'll just thank you. I'd like to frame it and give it to Lucas for our anniversary." Her cheeks were a little pinker than usual. "Perhaps it's vain, giving him a likeness of myself, but I think he'd like it."

Dixie smiled. "You'll be giving him a picture of someone at the center of his life. Of course he'll like it." She closed the pad. "I'll need to hang on to it until I've finished the painting, though."

"Our anniversary isn't for another two months. No rush." Caroline stood. "I take it you're through with me?"

"For now," Dixie said cheerfully. "I'll be starting the paintings soon, and I may need to stare at you some more then. Or not. First I'm going to pester your vineyard foreman for a day or two."

"I suspect Russ won't mind," Caroline said dryly. "Dixie?"

She slid her pad into her tote. "Yes?"

"My son was deeply hurt when you left him. I'm concerned about your reappearance in his life."

Dixie froze. *Déjà vu, all over again,* she thought. First Eli, now Caroline.

And what could she say? That Cole was the one doing the pursuing? It was true, but if she was honest, she'd have to admit she enjoyed the game they were playing. "I don't know what to tell you. He isn't serious."

"Isn't he?" Caroline let that question dangle a moment, then smiled. "You probably want to suggest I mind my own business. I understand. We'll change the subject. I'm having a small dinner party Friday, mostly family. I'd like it if you could join us."

"Thank you," Dixie said, wary.

Caroline shook her head ruefully. "I'm not usually so maladroit. The dinner invitation has nothing to do with the question I didn't quite ask you. Truly, I would like to have you join us."

"And I'm not usually so prickly." Dixie's smile warmed. "I'd love to come."

"Head over any time after six, then. Casual dress. We'll eat around seven-thirty."

Dixie was frowning as she headed for the carriage house. She didn't resent Caroline's delicate prying. Mothers were allowed to worry—it was in the contract. They were also entitled to think the best of their offspring. Dixie couldn't very well tell Cole's mother that all he was after was a quick roll in the hay.

Well…maybe not quick. Her lips curved. That had never been one of Cole's faults.

Her smile didn't last. She suspected his pursuit rose, in part, from the desire to prove that he was over her. If that thought pinched a bit, she could understand it. Because Caroline had been right about the other. Dixie was sure she'd hurt Cole.

He'd hurt her, too. But his had been sins of omission, not commission. He hadn't lied or cheated. He just hadn't *been* there enough. Business had come first, second and sometimes third with Cole. All too often, Dixie had been an afterthought.

She'd been so desperately in love. And he…he'd been halfway in love. In the end, she hadn't been able to handle that.

Dixie rounded the corner of the house—and almost walked right into Cole. And her cat, who was purring madly in Cole's arms.

"Good grief." She shook her head, disgusted. "He got out again?"

"I was working on a budget projection and turned away to get a file. When I turned back, there he was, sitting on top of a stack of quarterly reports, cleaning his face and looking smug. Tilly's still hiding under my desk. Hey." He touched her arm lightly with his free hand. "Is something wrong?"

"Just thinking deep, philosophical thoughts. It interferes with my digestion." She started walking again. He fell into step beside her. "Is Tilly okay?"

"She's fine, now that I removed her tormenter." He smiled. "That's three, Dixie. And still two days to go."

"I know, I know." She and Cole had a bet on. Cole had bet that Hulk would escape at least half a dozen times before Friday.

It should have been an easy win for her. Not because she fooled herself that she controlled Hulk, but she did know his ways. She'd figured her cat would escape once a day, no matter what she did—but if she let him stay out long enough to get his outside fix, he'd be content to stay in the rest of the time.

She hadn't counted on his obsession with Cole's dog. "I think you're sneaking him out," she said darkly.

"Would I do that? He may be teleporting. Here." Cole dumped the cat into her arms. "Where did you find Cattila the Hun, anyway?"

Had Cole always had this deliciously wry sense of humor, and she'd forgotten? "He just showed up one day, sitting outside my apartment as if he'd been waiting for me. I opened the door and he strolled in, demanded dinner, then curled up in my lap and informed me it was time to pet him."

Cole nodded. "I can see where you wouldn't want to argue with him."

"He was half-starved."

"He's made up for it." There was a hint of the devil in his sidelong glance. "Maybe I should borrow his technique. As I recall, you're a great cook. If I show up demanding dinner—"

She laughed. "You won't get in the door. I suspect your priorities are different from Hulk's."

"You're right." His voice dropped as he stroked her arm. "I'd want to go straight to the petting."

Just that light touch, and her system hummed happily. She wanted more, and there was no one around but herself to warn her of the dangers. "Hands off. I can't defend myself with my arms full of Hulk."

"I know. I like you helpless."

"You've never seen me helpless," she retorted. They'd reached the carriage house. "Open the door, will you, so I can put my monster back where he belongs."

Instead he leaned against the door, smiling. "Bribe me."

"Oh, come on, Cole—"

"Just a kiss. I'll even promise to keep my hands

to myself." But he wasn't. He'd reached for a strand of her hair and was tickling her with it—under her chin, along her throat. "One kiss...or don't you dare?"

She raised an eyebrow even as a shiver touched her spine. "You think I'm juvenile enough to jump at that bait?"

"I can hope." He moved even closer, stopping with scant inches between them. The heat of his body seemed to set the air between them ashimmer with possibilities. "Why not, Dixie? It's not as if you don't want to kiss me."

Her heart was pounding. "Your neck ever get tired from holding up that swollen head of yours?"

He just smiled. "It's only a kiss. What could it hurt?"

*All kinds of things—me, you...*but apparently she wasn't very good at listening to herself, because she went up on tiptoe, pausing with her lips a breath away from his. "No hands," she murmured. And she kissed him. Slowly. Just a skimming of lips at first...

"Uh-uh," she said when he tried to take over. "This one's mine."

Hulk was between them, so their bodies didn't touch. Just their mouths. The scent of him was a heady intimacy as she tickled his bottom lip with her tongue, then touched it to each corner of his mouth, and arousal was pure pleasure. The ache grew, gradually focusing like a perspective drawing, when all lines lead to a single point.

Dixie opened her mouth over his and took his breath inside her—which was just as well, for she didn't seem to have enough of her own. For a moment they met fully, lips, tongues, breath.

Then she eased back, smiling. And was pleased by the stunned look on his face.

He reached for her. She stepped back, shaking her head. "No hands, remember? Open the door, Cole."

"The door." He blinked. "Right. Anything you say. Sure you wouldn't like all my worldly goods instead?"

"Not just now, thanks." She sauntered inside, still holding her cat…with her heart pounding and pounding, and a little voice inside asking if she'd lost her mind.

This had to be about the stupidest thing he'd ever done, Grant thought as he gunned his pickup in order to keep up with the shiny blue Mercedes half a block ahead on the busy highway. He was acting like some two-bit private eye, for crying out loud.

But Grant didn't give up easily. Some called him pigheaded. He preferred to think of himself as determined. And so far, Spencer Ashton had refused to see him, leaving Grant only two options: give up and go home, or somehow force the bastard to talk to him.

The bastard who'd fathered him. His father. Grant forced himself to use the word, though it went down about as well as ground glass.

Looked as if they were heading out of the city. Spencer owned a big, fancy mansion near Napa. If that's where he was going, Grant was out of luck. He'd already been turned away from that door. From the high-rise office building here in San Francisco where Spencer went most mornings, too.

Which is why Grant was playing P.I. Sooner or later the man would go someplace where none of his servants or employees manned the gates.

Sooner or later his *father* would have to speak to him.

Grant scowled. More than once he'd wished he'd never seen that damn TV show. He'd come in from working on the older of his two tractors, showered and settled down with a cold beer. The game hadn't started yet, so he'd been thinking about the weather while some documentary about winemaking finished up. A perky young reporter had been interviewing Spencer Ashton of Ashton-Lattimer, a corporation that owned vineyards and a large commercial winery.

Ashton Estate Winery. The name had snagged Grant's attention, naturally, since it matched his own surname. But it was the face that had riveted him.

Spencer Ashton's face looked like the one he saw in the mirror every day. Not in any one feature, maybe, but something about the way they were grouped. That had been spooky, but it hadn't occurred to Grant the man might be his father. Even though the names were the same, he'd known it was impossible. His father had died when he was barely a year old.

Then the interviewer had mentioned Spencer's

Nebraska upbringing. They'd flashed a picture of him as a young man—and the man in that photo had been identical to the one standing beside Grant's mother in the yellowed wedding photo she'd kept by her bed until the day she died.

Two weeks later, Grant had climbed in his pickup and started for San Francisco, leaving Ford in charge at the farm.

Ford had asked what he expected to accomplish. Grant had told his nephew he wanted to meet the half brothers and half sisters he'd never known existed. That was true, if only a partial truth.

So far he hadn't mustered the nerve. He'd driven out to The Vines one morning, but hadn't been able to bring himself to ring the doorbell. It was weird to walk up to a bunch of strangers and say, "Hi, I'm your brother." Their money complicated matters. They were likely to think he wanted something from them.

He did, but it had nothing to do with money. Family mattered. These strangers were family. He needed to know what they were like.

What he hadn't told Ford was that he also needed to look the man who'd fathered him in the eye and say, "You can't pretend I don't exist. I do."

What good that would do, he couldn't say. But he was going to do it. Maybe today, maybe later, but he wasn't leaving California until he did.

On Friday, Cole took Dixie to Charley's restaurant in Yountville for lunch.

"I can't believe I let you finagle me into this," Dixie said, sliding out of Cole's suvvy.

"You lost the bet." Cole was entirely too pleased with himself.

"That part I understand. How I let you talk me into making such a dumb bet, I don't."

"Maybe you didn't really want to win." He held the door for her.

"I knew you were going to say that. The fact is, Hulk's gone over to the Dark Side. He conspired with you."

"You're talking about a cat, Dixie."

"I'm talking about Hulk."

"I get your point. Table for two," he told the hostess. "I have a reservation."

"Of course, Mr. Ashton. This way."

Dixie raised her eyebrows. "They know you here."

"We sell them wine."

She nodded. "And just when did you make that reservation?"

"The same day we made the bet, of course."

Dixie wouldn't have admitted it for anything, but she was glad she'd lost the bet. Charley's had been around awhile, but she couldn't afford the place back when she lived here before and somehow she'd never made it here on her visits home.

The restaurant was set on twelve acres of olive groves, vineyards and gardens brimming with seasonal flowers, herbs and vegetables. Most of the herbs and produce used in their dishes came out of the ground the same day it was cooked. Plus they had an exhibition kitchen.

Dixie considered cooking every bit as much of an art as painting. She was looking forward to watching the pros at work.

"I've been thinking," Cole said after the manager stopped by to welcome them. "If I'd lost the bet, I would have had to donate money to a charity of your choice. Having won the bet, I'm still spending money. What's wrong with this picture?"

She chuckled. "You set the terms, not me."

He shook his head. "What was I thinking?"

As they debated their selections, Dixie admitted to herself that she wasn't just enjoying the place. She was enjoying the man. Had she had this much pure fun with Cole before?

All week, the present had been poking holes in the preconceptions of the past. Dixie remembered an ambitious, rather grim young man who'd had little time to spare for anything except business. This Cole was intense, yes, but he possessed a keen sense of the ridiculous. Even his pursuit of her had been flavored with humor.

And that, she told herself as she placed her order, was more dangerous than a sexual buzz, however potent. She had to be on her guard…because she was beginning to hope. She was trying not to define that hope, but it fizzed around inside, a giddy effervescence that bubbled up into smiles and easy laughter.

Cole selected the wine—one from another vineyard, so he could see what the competition was up to, he said. She picked the entrées. They argued about home schooling, sushi and a recent action movie, and found themselves agreeing about reality TV, garlic and childproof safety caps.

Dixie had a wonderful time until the waiter took their desert orders and left. All at once, Cole's face froze.

"What is it?" she asked.

"Nothing." He was staring over her shoulder in a way that should have turned whoever he was looking at into a Popsicle.

She craned her head around. A small knot of people blocked the entrance. Her eyebrows rose. She recognized one of them—the Western-looking man who'd been wandering around the vineyard earlier that week. The manager seemed upset with him.

The other two she'd never seen before, yet she recognized one. Not the curvy blonde in the red power suit. The older man resting a possessive hand on her back.

He had silver hair and an impeccably tailored suit over a lean body. His eyebrows were straight, his nose strong, his small, neat ears set flat to his head. His features were symmetrical, possessing the kind of balance people call handsome in a man, beauty in a woman.

He looked exactly like Cole would in another thirty years.

"Dammit, Dixie, don't stare." Cole's voice was low and angry. "He doesn't matter."

That was blatantly false, so she ignored it. "That's your father, isn't it?"

"My real dad is married to my mother. That man is nothing. Nothing at all."

The problem, whatever it was, appeared to be resolved. The manager was escorting Western Man out of the restaurant—and one of the waiters was leading Cole's father and the woman with him their way.

The woman's hair woke envy in Dixie's heart. It was long, pale blond with a hint of curl. Her situation didn't. She looked as if she didn't appreciate the hand resting on her back. And the man escorting her didn't seem to know his son existed.

The waiter stopped at their table, looking flustered. "My apologies, sir. There's been some mistake. This table is reserved."

"I know," Cole said in his refrigerator voice. "I reserved it."

"But…I'm terribly sorry, sir, but this is Mr. Ashton's table."

"Good. I'm glad we agree."

The poor waiter didn't know what to say. Nothing Man was too bored and important to wrangle in public, and besides was busy pretending he didn't see his son sitting there. The woman with him looked too uncomfortable to do anything to defuse the situation. She even took a small step away, maybe distancing herself from the looming scene, maybe ditching that possessive hand. And Cole wasn't about to make anything easier for anyone, including himself.

So Dixie took over. She smiled at the waiter. "There's a misunderstanding, but it's easily cleared up. There are two Mr. Ashtons present. That, I believe, is Mr. Spencer Ashton." She nodded at Cole's father, eyebrows raised. "Aren't you?"

He was faintly surprised, as if a chair had addressed him. "Yes, I am. And this is my assistant, Kerry Roarke. You are—?"

"Dixie McCord." She turned her smile up a notch. "And this is your son, Cole Ashton."

Cole choked and began coughing.

The manager came rushing up. "Idiot. Idiot." That seemed to be addressed to the waiter. "Go away. I'll handle this. I am so terribly sorry," he said, spreading his hands to include both Mr. Ashtons in the apology. "We have your table, of course, Mr. Ashton." A small nod indicated the older man. "It's right over here. If you'll follow me—?"

As soon as they were out of earshot Cole said, "If you think I'm going to thank you for that bit of interference—"

"I'm not that naive. I suppose you want to leave now that you've defended your territory."

He stood and tossed his napkin on the table.

Dixie ached for him. Not one word had his father spoken to him. There hadn't been even a glance—no curiosity, nothing. *Nothing Man is a good name for him,* she thought as Cole scattered a few bills on the table.

She knew better than to let Cole see how she hurt for him. Hold out a hand in sympathy right now and he'd snap it off. The walls he'd pulled behind were steep and silent—but then, he had a lot of anger for them to hold back.

It began spilling out when they got in his suvvy. "Did you see that bimbo with him? His *assistant*." He made the word sound obscene. "Doesn't look like he's changed his habits."

"I don't think she's a bimbo." Dixie fastened her seat belt. It looked as if they were in for a rough ride.

"Bimbo, mistress, what's the difference?" He backed out, slammed the car into Drive and stepped on the gas. "I wonder if Bimbo Number One knows about Bimbo Number Two."

Bimbo Number One, she assumed, would be his stepmother, the woman Spencer Ashton had had an affair with. The one he'd married as soon as the divorce from Cole's mother was final. The woman he'd raised a second family with—a family he hadn't deserted. "There may be nothing to know. I don't think that woman is his mistress," Dixie repeated patiently. "The body language was wrong."

"Oh, he's staked a claim there, all right." Cole swung out onto the street with barely a pause. "Trust me on that."

"He may be staking a claim, but she hasn't accepted it."

"Don't be naive. She was uncomfortable at being spotted with him by his son. Probably didn't realize I'm from his *other* family—the one he doesn't see, speak to or give two cents about."

Dixie decided they had better things to fight about

than a woman they'd never see again. "You are not like him, Cole."

"Where did that come from?" He was cutting through traffic as if he needed to be somewhere, anywhere, other than where he was right now. "You don't know what the hell you're talking about."

"You look like him. That doesn't mean you're *like* him."

"I don't want to talk about it."

"Okay. We'll save it for when you aren't driving."

"There's nothing wrong with my driving."

She rolled her eyes. "If you want to argue, fine. But you don't get to pick the subject."

"And you do, I suppose?"

"Yes, because you'd have us fighting about all the wrong things. What you really need to fight about—"

"I told you I don't want to talk about him."

At least Cole had moved close enough to the real subject to say "him" instead of "it." Dixie decided to let him hole up inside his turbulence until he wasn't behind the wheel, so she said nothing.

Neither did he. The silence held until she noticed which way they were heading. "This is not the way to The Vines."

"I need to drive for a while. It clears my head."

"You have a destination in mind, or are we just going to dodge traffic?"

"My cabin."

Six

Cole spent the drive to his cabin caught up in a whirlwind of thoughts and feelings. When would he be old enough for it to stop mattering? So what if his father was a sorry sonofabitch? Millions of people had lousy fathers. He ought to be able to shrug off the bastard's indifference by now.

Most of the time he could. He did. Today, though…there was just something about seeing Spencer with his newest side piece, pulling the same shit that had wrecked Cole's life all those years ago. It rubbed him raw, too, that Dixie had been there. He didn't know why. It just did.

If he hadn't looked up to the man so much when he was a kid, tried so hard to win his approval…

The past was a closed book, he reminded himself, pulling to a stop in front of his cabin. Put it back on the shelf and leave it alone. "Go on inside," he told Dixie, climbing out. "I'm going to chop some wood."

"Oh, good idea," she said, getting out and shutting her door. "Go play with an ax while you're too mad too see straight. I'll get the bandages and tourniquet ready."

He flicked one glance at her then walked away, heading for the edge.

The cabin was surrounded on three sides by oak, pine and brush, but the strip along the front was clear all the way to the drop-off. There, the land fell away in dizzying folds. The view always opened him up, made him breathe easier.

It didn't do a damn thing for him today. He stopped a pace back from the rocky edge and shoved his hands in his pockets.

Dixie had followed him, of course. "This would be easier if you really were Sheila. I can't help you vent in the traditional male way, by getting into a fistfight."

"I should have known all that silence was too good to last."

"If you wanted silence, you should have come here alone."

Why hadn't he? He was in no mood for company, yet it hadn't occurred to him to take her back to The Vines before heading here. "If you wanted me to drop you off, you should have said something."

"I'm just putting you on notice. You brought me along. Now you have to put up with me."

"I want to show you the cabin." There. He knew he'd had a reason for bringing her. "But I need a minute to myself first."

"You need to do something with all the stuff churning around inside you, all right. Try talking."

"I'm not in the mood for amateur therapy."

"You know, people were talking—sometimes even listening—for a few thousand years before Freud called it therapy."

He gave her an ugly look. "You won't let it be, will you? You have to poke and prod and try to fix me."

"I used to do that. It was a mistake."

His eyebrows went up. "You're admitting it?"

"Astonishing, isn't it? But I wasn't the only one. We both tried to fix each other. Your technique was a little different, that's all." She shrugged. "Young and stupid sums it up, I guess. We fell hard and immediately started trying to change each other into people it would be safer to love."

Love. The word scraped across places already raw. "You found plenty that needed fixing, didn't you? There wasn't that much that you liked about me back then."

She winced. "I can see where you got that impression, but it isn't true. There was plenty I liked. And," she admitted, "one or two things I couldn't live with."

She'd made that plain. Restless, he started walking. "Why did you come back, Dixie?"

She fell into step with him. "You keep asking me that."

He didn't know what kind of answer he was looking for. Just that he hadn't gotten it yet.

What was wrong with him, anyway? He'd planned to bring Dixie to his cabin after lunch—but he'd been hoping for a little afternoon delight, not a session mucking around in his least pleasant memories. Not to mention his least pleasant self. "I'm acting like an idiot, aren't I? Sorry." He made himself smile.

She stopped. "Don't do that."

"Don't do what? Be pleasant? Polite?"

"Don't put on a happy face for me."

"What if it isn't for you?" he snapped. "Maybe I need to remind myself I can be civilized."

She stood there, shoulders straight, eyes narrowed as she studied him. God, he used to love the way she faced off with him, not backing down an inch... Cole took a deep breath. Some things it was best not to remember too clearly. "Walk with me a bit, okay?"

"Okay." And that was all she said.

Cole headed for one of his favorite paths, a deer trail that led to a small meadow that was green and pretty now. It would be spectacular in the spring, he thought. Dixie would love it when the wildflowers burst into bloom.

But she wouldn't be here in the spring, would she?

Carpe the damn *diem*, then. If all he had was another week or so, he'd better make the most of them. "What did you think of my cabin? I realize you haven't seen much of it yet."

"I love it. But it wasn't what I'd been expecting."

"What were you expecting?"

The path was too narrow for them to walk abreast, so she was following him. He couldn't see her teasing smile, but he heard it in her voice. "Something more rustic. A *lot* more rustic. You did say you'd done a lot of the work yourself."

"You lack confidence in my carpentry."

"I didn't think you knew one end of a saw from the other."

"I didn't, to start out with," he admitted. "After the wall fell down, I took a couple courses."

She laughed. "It really fell down? Which one?"

As he told her the story of his early, botched attempt at fixing up his place, a wave of relief swept through him. They'd be okay. As long as they kept it light, didn't let things get intense, they'd be fine.

At the end of the tree-shrouded path lay his meadow. His heart lifted as he stepped from shade to sun. There was nothing vast or magnificent about this spot. The beauties here were small and common, but something about the shape of the pocket-size meadow seemed to cup the sunshine, to gather and soften it. He could have sworn the grass grew a little greener here, waving gently in a breeze the trees had blocked. Off to the west a towhee called its name—*to-whee, to-whee*.

"Oh…" Dixie stopped several paces behind him

and turned in a slow circle. "A little piece of perfection, isn't it?"

Her response pleased him. "This is the other reason I bought the place."

"It's lovely." She stood motionless and smiling, glossed by sunshine. The breeze teased her hair and pressed her thin blue dress against a shape that was pure female.

Longing hit, a sweep of emotion that made him feel larger, lighter, full of air and dreams…then receded, leaving him mute and unsteady.

"Cole?" She tilted her head. "Is something wrong?"

"Probably." He'd been wrong. Terribly wrong. He didn't want a few days of friendly, keep-it-light sex from her. He wanted more. Much more.

He walked slowly up to her.

Nerves flickered in her eyes. She knew what was on his mind, oh yes. She didn't back up—but she wanted to, he could see that. Instead she tilted her head back, frowning. "What flipped your switch?"

"You." He put his hands on her arms and ran them up to her shoulders, letting the warmth of her seep into his palms. "You always have."

"I don't think this—"

"Good. Don't think." He crushed his mouth down on hers.

She jolted. He knew that, but only dimly—the ripe taste of her flooded him, a wine more heady than sweet. He pulled her tight against him, running his hands over her, feeding on the feel of her, the scent and taste and heat that was Dixie.

It wasn't enough. He needed more—needed enough of her that she wouldn't leave, couldn't leave him again. His arms tightened around her.

And, dammit to hell, as soon as he did that, she started struggling. Pushing him away.

Cole had to drop his arms and let her go. Again. And it hurt, again.

Her mouth was wet, her hair wildly mussed and her eyes snapping with anger. "I won't be forced."

It was guilt that made him snap back. "Forced? It was a kiss!"

"You were going too fast. Pushing too hard."

His mouth twisted. So did something inside, something that spilled out ugliness. "You've given me every reason to think you'd like to be kissed. Or was that all part of the game? Do you get a charge out of teasing men?"

"Where did that come from?" she snapped.

"You like men, don't you? Eli, Russ, me—you flirt with us all. Am I just one of your men, Dixie?"

She spun around and started back toward the path.

"That's right. Walk away. That's your answer to everything."

She paused. Slowly she turned. "People who leave aren't exactly high on your list, are they, Cole? Or maybe they make the wrong list. Eleven years ago, I was the one to leave. We haven't talked about that."

"That's right, I forgot. Talking is your other answer."

She scowled. "I like yelling, too, sometimes."

"I remember." God, he did remember. Not the exact words of that last fight, but the feelings. She'd been furious, hurt—and the more angry she'd gotten, the colder he'd turned, until he'd thought he might never be warm again. "You yelled plenty when I forgot your birthday. Then you left me."

She stared. "Tell me that isn't the way you remember it."

"It's what happened! I messed up with the dates—"

"You refused to change a dinner with a client to another day!" She advanced, fists clenched at her sides. "We had a date, you and I, but you forgot and booked a dinner with a client for that night. I was hurt, yes, because you'd forgotten, but that wasn't why I left!"

"Then why?" he demanded. "Tell me why, because I remember you screaming at me that if I wouldn't take you out instead of my client, you were leaving—and you did!"

"You could have switched your client to another night instead of putting me off! I came last, like usual. Over and over you showed me where I stood—business came first, your family second, and I finished a poor third. Yet in spite of that, you couldn't stand it if I so much as smiled at another man!"

His lip curled. "Half the time, you smiled at everyone but me. Is it any wonder I wasn't sure of you?"

"You weren't there for me to smile at! God, I'd

be waiting for a phone call, then when it came you'd tell me you had to cancel lunch. Or dinner. By the last month we were together," she finished bitterly, "you'd canceled pretty much everything except sex. That, you had time for."

Her words struck him mute, inside and out. In the flash of mental silence that followed he heard his own words, past and present, echoing in his mind. After a moment he asked quietly, "Did you really think that? That all I wanted from you was sex?"

She gave her head a little shake, as if she were emerging from the fog, too. When she spoke there was a thread of humor in her voice. "Surely I must have screamed something along those lines."

"By then we were accusing each other of every-thing short of abetting the Holocaust. I didn't think you meant it."

"I, on the other hand, believed you meant every word. You weren't screaming, like me. You were deep in your chill zone, still speaking in complete, grammatically correct sentences…everything you said came out cold and deliberate."

"I have no idea what I said. I was terrified."

Her eyebrows shot up. "You?"

"Oh, yeah. I was losing you and I knew it." He'd never really believed he'd be able to hold on to her, so he'd held on too tightly, letting jealousy twist its knife in him. "I'd bought a ring."

The words just slipped out. Dammit, he'd never wanted her to know that, never wanted anyone to re-alize how deep and complete a fool he'd been.

Her eyes went huge. "A ring?" she whispered.

"I was going to ask you to wear it on your birthday. Or," he added wryly, "on whatever night I managed to make time to celebrate your birthday."

Her eyes closed. She rubbed her chest as if it hurt. "Give me a minute. You… That's a real leveler." She paced away a few steps, then just stood there, her hand on her chest, looking away…pretty far away, he suspected. About eleven years. "If I'd known…"

"You might not have left. And that," he added with painful honesty, "would probably have been a mistake. I wanted to keep you, but I had no intention of changing. I didn't know how, back then. We'd have made each other miserable."

She looked back at him. "I was sure you'd call. I waited for weeks for you to call and say you'd been wrong and wanted me back."

"I was waiting for you to call and apologize. I gave you a month, being big on tests back then. You mentioned that." He remembered only too well what she'd said. "Or shouted it. You were sick of the way I kept testing you, but as usual I didn't listen. At the end of the month I decided you'd failed the test. I pitched the ring into the deepest canyon I could find. It was all very dramatic."

She shook her head, a sad smile touching her mouth. "God have mercy on the young."

"Young and stupid," he agreed. "Both of us."

Suddenly she laughed. "Pigheaded fits, too. Both of us waiting for the other one to call—"

"Confess their sins—"

"And come crawling back." She grinned. "Admit it. The crawling part figured in your fantasies, too."

"Absolutely." Right up until he threw away the ring that had meant so much…and so little. After that, he'd made up his mind to forget her.

He'd failed.

For a moment they just looked at each other, letting the past settle back into place. Cole found that the shapes it fell into weren't quite the ones it had held before. "I was out of line earlier," he admitted. "Way out. I shouldn't have accused you of being a tease, or…" He swallowed. "Or forced a kiss you didn't want."

"I wanted it," she said, low voiced. "Then I got scared."

"God, I never meant—"

"Of course not," she said quickly. "If I'd let you know…but I don't like to admit it when I'm frightened."

But he knew of another time she'd been frightened, one she'd told him about. That knowledge hung between them.

She'd been eight when her father died, fifteen when her mother became engaged again. Helen McCord had believed she'd found the man who would take care of her and her daughter forever. Dixie hadn't liked him, but she'd kept quiet about it for her mother's sake. They'd just moved in together when Helen's heart condition had grown suddenly worse. She'd gone in for surgery, comforted by the knowledge that the man she loved would be there to take care of her daughter.

The day after her surgery, that man had cornered Dixie in her bedroom. She'd gotten away. She'd even left her mark—the bastard probably bore a scar on his forehead to this day. And she hadn't told her mother about it until Helen was home from rehab.

It was typical of Dixie. Admirable. And it provided a stark exclamation point to all the reasons he'd had for doubting she could ever commit completely to one man. Life had taught her not to trust men. To rely only on herself.

"It wasn't you I was afraid of," Dixie said at last. "Not you. That doesn't mean you're off the hook for your comments," she added with attempted lightness. "Some women may find jealousy attractive. I don't."

"Noted." He nodded, grimly accepting that he'd given her a flashback moment. One more in a long series of mistakes he'd made with her. "You've seen my temper, my favorite spot and my least favorite side of myself. Can I show you my cabin now?"

She shook her head. "I do want to see it, but not today. Things are pretty charged between us right now. I don't want to fall into your bed by accident."

His pulse leaped. *Down, boy,* he told his most optimistic body part, and held out a hand. "Walk back with me?"

She smiled, came to him and took his hand. The connection felt good. After a moment he said, "I guess this means I'll have to postpone my plans for an afternoon of hot sex."

Her laugh was shaky. "Good guess."

Postponed, he thought. What a wonderful word. For a few minutes it had looked as if he was going to lose her all over again. They walked back in a silence every bit as complete as when they'd walked out to the meadow…and wholly different.

Seven

It was surprisingly easy to keep the conversation light on the way back to The Vines. Maybe, Dixie thought, because of that stubborn rascal, hope. It was back, messing with her mind, making her think dangerous thoughts.

She reminded herself that they hadn't really settled anything. Certainly nothing inside her felt settled. Cole had toppled several of her fixed ideas about the past, turning the present into unfamiliar territory.

He'd bought her a ring. He'd been planning to ask her to wear it.

Never, not once, had she dreamed that Cole had given any thought to marriage. He'd wanted more than one summer, yes. He'd urged her to take a job in San Francisco so they could continue their affair. She probably would have, too, even though the New York job she'd been offered was better for her professionally. If not for their last big fight she probably would have stayed in California to be close to him.

What if Cole had taken her out, as planned, on her birthday? What if he'd presented her with that ring? Would she have said yes?

She didn't know. That unsettled Dixie more deeply than anything else she'd learned today. For years she'd thought of herself as the one deeply in love, the one most hurt when they couldn't make their relationship work…now she learned that Cole had been ready to commit to her for life. And she wasn't sure if she would have said yes.

Shouldn't she *know?* If she'd been so deeply in love, why hadn't she thought about marriage?

Dixie couldn't find answers for those questions. Maybe it was impossible to see the past clearly through the lens of the present. After all, the woman who'd loved Cole for that short, mad summer was gone.

But the woman who remembered that summer was sitting beside a man who tempted her in ways the younger Cole hadn't. Hope and humor were beguilements she didn't know how to defend against.

Maybe she didn't want to.

By the time they reached The Vines, the sky was grumbling to itself through stacked-up clouds dark with rain. Dixie was congratulating herself on arriving ahead of the storm when she noticed the two unfamiliar cars in front of the big house.

She groaned. "I forgot about the dinner tonight. Should I change? Cancel that," she said with a glance at her watch. "There isn't time." She started digging in her purse, hoping she'd remembered her lipstick.

Cole grinned. "If I say you look fine, am I being supportive or insensitive?"

"Honest, I hope." No lipstick. She grimaced and took out the little brush. At least she could get rid of the tangles.

He got out, came around to her side and opened her door. She finished with her hair, stashed the brush, stepped out—and he took her hands, both of them, carried them to his mouth and pressed a kiss to the back of each, in turn. "Fine doesn't begin to cover it," he said softly. "I'm not sure how to tell you how good you look."

Her cheeks warmed with pleasure. "Try."

He cocked one wicked eyebrow. "I could say you look like a wet dream."

She laughed and pulled her hands back. "Not when I'm going to dinner with your folks, you can't." She slanted him a mischievous look. "But it's okay if you think it."

"I'm thinking," he assured her as they headed for the door.

The living room lay past the foyer and the gallery with its curving staircase, and opened onto the covered lanai where Dixie had sketched Caroline. It was a cheerful blend of antiques and French country accents, with fabrics ranging from the drapes striped in poppy, grass and sunflower to the chairs covered in poppy-and-black toiles.

At the moment, it was full of tense people. One of them was the man Dixie had seen twice now. The Western Man.

She stopped three paces in, astonished and wary. Whatever he was doing here, no one looked very happy about it.

Mercedes stood near the sofa with her boyfriend *du jour,* Craig Bradford—who must have some virtues Dixie had failed to discover, since he'd lasted longer than most. Good looks alone weren't enough to account for that, given her friend's theories about relationships.

Merry looked stunned. Her sister, Jillian, sat on the couch, staring at the stranger and shaking her head slowly, as if she were denying some monstrous question. Across from them, standing nearest their visitor, was Eli.

Eli was furious.

It wasn't obvious, but Dixie had studied that face. She saw the rigid control in the muscles along his jaw and the emotion seething in eyes that burned like green fire.

They all had green eyes, all of Spencer Ashton's children, didn't they?

Dixie's mouth fell open at a sudden, impossible thought. Her gaze swung to the stranger.

"What's going on?" Cole asked, his voice sharp.

Eli's gaze swung to him. "Let me introduce you. This is Grant *Ashton*. Your oldest brother."

"So he says." Merry's voice was flat.

Oh, yes, Dixie thought. Yes, the head shape was the same. The eyes. She'd seen the resemblance the morning she ran into him, but it hadn't occurred to her...

"What the hell—?" Cole's words were more question than curse. He looked from one to the other of them.

"I know this must be a shock. I'm sorry for that." That was the stranger, Western Man...Grant Ashton.

Cole took a step forward, his face hard. "You'd better have some sort of proof."

"He does." Caroline Ashton stood in the doorway to the kitchen, her face pale but composed. "He showed me his parents' marriage license."

"You spoke to him?" Eli asked, scowling.

She nodded. "I'm sorry. I should have been here when he told you. I...he arrived half an hour ago. After I spoke with him, I went to call Lucas. He's on his way back from the city and would have been here soon anyway, but I...I just wanted to talk to him. I should have been here," she repeated. "I'm sorry."

"Never mind that." Jillian hurried to her mother's side. "Are you all right?"

Caroline smiled. "Of course."

"I wasn't going to tell them until you returned," Grant said. "But your daughter found me waiting for you in the lanai and insisted I join the family in here. She was trying to be hospitable to a guest, I suppose," he said wryly. "Then your son asked my name. I wasn't going to make one up."

"No, of course not. And once you told them you were an Ashton, you had to tell them the rest."

"What's the rest?" Cole demanded.

Grant met his eyes levelly. "My parents married young—a shotgun wedding, you might say. People still do that where I come from, or did, back when my mother found out she was pregnant. Until a couple weeks ago, I thought my father died when I was a year old. Turns out he just took off, leaving my mother to raise me and my sister." He paused. "My father's name is Spencer Ashton."

No one moved. No one spoke. Then Cole's sharp bark of laughter broke the silence. "The bastard started young, didn't he?"

Caroline insisted that Grant join them for dinner. It was an awkward meal.

Merry was withdrawn, mostly silent. Jillian was tense. Dixie had noticed that she was sensitive to others' moods, and the overall mood at the table that night was not jolly. Eli barely spoke—and Cole spoke too much, considering that he substituted grilling their guest for polite conversation.

They learned that Grant was from Crawley, Nebraska; that he had a farm there, which his nephew was running while he was gone; that he'd never married, but had raised his niece and nephew; and that he'd tried repeatedly to speak to Spencer, but the man brushed him off.

"I saw you at Charley's," Cole said. "You were trying to talk to him then?"

Grant nodded and buttered a roll.

"I can see why you'd think he owes you something, and he has plenty of money. Are you hoping to—"

"Cole!" Caroline said sharply. "That is quite enough."

"For the record," Grant said levelly, "I do fine, financially. I don't want anything from him. Or you."

Dixie gave him an approving smile. "For the record, Cole isn't always such an ass. It sneaks up on him occasionally."

Mercedes stifled a giggle. Cole turned to Dixie. "Thank you," he said, dry enough to suck the juice from a mummy, "for your unquestioning support."

"Friends don't let friends talk junk. Especially at their mother's table. Why don't we discuss something innocuous for a while, like religion or politics?"

Surprisingly, it was Craig who came to her rescue. "How about sports? I missed the game last Monday and have been hearing about the Patriots' fumble all week."

Lucas picked up that ball and ran with it, and they managed to stagger on through dessert. Dixie saw that Craig had at least one undeniable virtue— he was socially adroit. He helped her keep the conversation going more than once during the interminable meal. So that was why Merry kept him around—he made the perfect fashion accessory.

Pretty to look at, great at small talk, no obvious vices.

Dixie promised herself to find time soon to have a little talk with Merry. But not tonight. They still had to navigate the postdinner shoals.

She was worried about Cole. He'd made an effort to be civil for the rest of the meal, but the anger simmering in him demanded some kind of outlet. There wasn't much she could do about it right now, though.

When they adjourned to the living room, the atmosphere wasn't as tense as it had been immediately following the big revelation. Caroline and Lucas had cornered Cole and were forcing him to discuss some business involving the new chardonnay. Eli was talking to Grant about farming with Mercedes listening in, and Jillian had stepped out of the room for the moment.

That left Dixie with Craig. Unfortunately, he chose that time to demonstrate why he was Mr. Right Now instead of Mr. Right.

They chatted lightly for a few minutes about generalities. Feeling the need to give credit where credit was due, she thanked him for helping out during dinner.

"Glad I could do it." He moved closer and spoke low, as if confiding in her. "Mercedes has some issues about her father. I admired the way you smoothed things over."

"Mmm." The jerk was trying to look down her dress. She frowned and shifted away slightly. "All of them have issues about Spencer, and with reason."

He nodded solemnly. "Learning that he had yet another family that he abandoned was bound to upset them."

"It wasn't Grant's fault, of course, but it's hard not to associate the messenger with the message."

"I'm fortunate," he said. "My father and I get along great. Are you planning to stay in California, Dixie? I hope so."

Uh-oh. "Probably. Is your family from around here?"

"They're in Frisco. But enough about families. I've been wanting to tell you how much I like your work." His voice turned caressing. "Being an unimaginative business grunt, I admire artists. They're so…unconventional. I'd like to get to know you better."

Hints weren't going to work. "Don't you think it's tacky to come on to me with Mercedes in the room?"

He just smiled and reached up to toy with her hair. "Mercedes and I have an understanding. She likes you. I like you. Where's the harm?"

Dixie sighed. "Coming at you from three o'-clock."

He blinked, confused. "What?"

Cole plucked Craig's wineglass from his hand. "Sorry you have to leave so early, Bradford." The glitter in his eyes did not resemble regret.

"I don't have to—"

"Yes, you do." Cole gripped Craig's elbow with one hand and passed the glass to Dixie. "I'll walk you to the door."

March him to the door was more like it. Craig might not have been the brightest bulb on the tree, but he wasn't stupid enough to protest or try to shrug off the hand propelling him to the front door.

Dixie caught Mercedes' eye across the room. Merry shrugged apologetically, which annoyed Dixie no end. Her friend shouldn't be apologizing for the jerk. She should be dumping him.

Definitely they needed to talk.

Cole came back alone. He didn't look satisfied—more like a volcano ready to erupt. His eyes were hot when he snapped at her, "You ought to know better than to flirt with that idiot."

"Hold on," Eli said. "Dixie didn't do anything."

Cole swung around. "You stay out of this."

"Okay," Dixie said, taking Cole's arm. "That's enough. You tried. You made a valiant effort, but it isn't working." She sent a smile around the room. "Sorry to eat and run, but Cole and I need to go jog or chop wood or something."

"It's pouring down rain!" Lucas protested.

"So we'll swim laps. Come on," she said, pulling on Cole's arm. "Your mother does not want you punching your brother in her living room. Either of your brothers. Or anyone else, for that matter."

Cole stared at her a moment, eyes narrowed. Then he nodded curtly, shook off her hand and headed for the door.

He opened it and looked over his shoulder. "Are you coming or not?"

"Coats," she said, delving into the closet. She

didn't have one with her, so she borrowed a raincoat of Merry's. She tossed Cole his windbreaker.

He shrugged into it impatiently. Then they stepped out into the rain.

Eight

Somewhere to the west, unseen in the murk, the sun was setting. There was no wind; the rain fell straight and cold. Dixie buttoned her borrowed raincoat and resigned herself to wet hair and ruined shoes. Cole was headed for the vineyards.

They tramped along the strip of barley planted between the vines, not touching. Halfway to the grove of olive trees he spoke abruptly. "I'm sorry. You weren't flirting."

"No, I wasn't. It isn't me you're mad at."

"I don't know what's wrong with me." He stopped, jammed his hands in his pockets and tilted his face up, letting the rain wash it. Then he shook his head like a dog, scattering more drops, and started walking again. "I've been flying off the handle all day, and for no good reason."

"You hate your father, and his existence has been shoved in your face today."

"He's old news."

"He abandoned you."

"I put all that out of my mind years ago. Lucas has been a father to me, and a good one."

"The problem with stuffing everything into a compartment labeled 'the past' is that the lid can get jarred off."

He gave a single harsh bark of a laugh. "True. Then the ugly spills out. And there's a lot of ugly."

"Whose ugliness are you talking about? Yours? Or your father's?"

"There's plenty to go around, but we'll stick with his for now." The rain had sleeked all the curl from Cole's hair, laying it flat against his skull. He tilted his face up slightly and let the rain wash over it. "He stole my mother's birthright."

A theft that had made Spencer a rich man. Caroline's father had been of the old school, unable to believe that a woman could run a major business. He'd left his shares of the Lattimer Corporation to his son-in-law, not his daughter. Less than a year later, Spencer had left Caroline. "I didn't think you wanted any part of Lattimer Corporation."

"Not now. Not when it's been his so long. I don't want a damned thing that's his."

Yet hate was just a deep, hard form of wanting. Cole wanted fiercely for his father to have been a different sort of person, or at least for Spencer to suffer as he'd caused others to suffer.

"It was during the divorce that he really put the screws to her," Cole went on bitterly.

"What happened then?"

"He grabbed what was left. Money, properties—everything except The Vines."

"But how? What judge would let him do that?"

"How else? Lies, threats and trickery. He told Mom he'd take us away from her if she fought him. He had people ready to testify that she used drugs."

"God," she murmured, rubbing her middle. "He does turn the stomach, doesn't he?"

He didn't say anything for several minutes, then burst out, "How does he do it? Are people like clothes to him? If you get tired of a shirt you throw it away. He gets tired of a family and he throws them away. They don't exist for him after that."

Dixie thought Spencer Ashton sounded like a classic narcissist. Other people weren't real for him, except as echoes or reflections of his own ego. "What was he like when you were little?"

"I thought he liked me." Cole snorted. "I was stupid, obviously, but…sometimes he was great. He used to ruffle my hair when I brought home a good report card and say, 'Way to go, kid.' But it was winning he liked, not me."

"Was he hard to please?"

"More like hard to predict. If things were going badly for him, we all stayed away. He'd take it out on us. But sometimes he'd make a big deal about us.

Birthdays, for example. He liked throwing parties. When I turned six he threw this big bash—clowns, balloons, pony rides for the kids, a catered picnic for their parents."

The faint, wistful tone in his voice tugged at her. She swallowed. "Do you think parties were another way to enhance his own image?"

He shrugged. "They were more about him than me, but I didn't see that as a kid. He didn't come to school stuff, either, but back then I thought important people like him were always busy."

He fell silent. Dixie walked with him, trying not to slide around too much in her slick-soled shoes. Her hair hung in wet rattails down her neck, dripping water beneath the collar of her raincoat. She tugged it to one side.

They reached the little grove of olive trees. It was darker here, but the trees offered some shelter. She stopped. "What about when he left? Kids often blame themselves when their parents break up."

"I don't remember blaming myself exactly, but…" He didn't look at her. "You had it right when you said I hated him. But until he left, I'd tried to be like him."

"You were a kid. You wanted to please your father, and the only thing that pleases a narcissist is his own reflection."

"And I made myself into a damn good reflection, didn't I?"

"No!" She seized his arm, making him turn and look at her. "Where did you get the idea you're like him?"

"Aside from looking in the mirror, you mean?" Rain ran down the taut lines of his face as if the sky were weeping for him. "Come on, Dixie. You're not dense. I've spent years building Louret up so I could prove to the bastard that we didn't need him. That I'm better than he is in the one way that means anything to him—making money."

"You're ambitious, yes. But you don't use people. You'd never discard someone the way he has."

"You left me because I was like him."

Dixie's breath caught, hard and painful, in her chest. Was that what he'd thought? All these years had he believed, deep down, that her leaving proved he was like his father?

"Cole." She reached up with both hands and cupped his hard, wet face between her hands, blinking back tears. "You idiot."

He searched her face. He couldn't have seen much in the dimness, but apparently he saw enough. He had no trouble finding her mouth with his.

His kiss was soft and slow and unbearably moving. He drifted his mouth over her cheek. "You're cold."

"No kidding." But it wasn't cold that made her shiver. It was his fingers playing along her throat.

He wrapped his arms around her and held on tight. "Warmer?" he murmured next to her ear, then kissed it.

She was cold, wet, muddy, and her heart was knocking against the wall of her chest so hard it was a wonder he couldn't hear it. From fear? Arousal? Sheer exhilaration?

Did it matter? She put her hands on his chest. "Not yet," she whispered, the words barely audible over the *shush-shush* of the rain. "Try harder."

This time his mouth meant business. He kissed, licked and sucked, keeping his arms wrapped tightly around her. Her hands were trapped against his chest. She couldn't move—could only tip her head back and meet his tongue with hers. His breath was warm. His body was warm and hard, and she ached.

She wiggled her arms loose, needing to feel the planes and angles and muscle of him. Sliding her hands under his jacket, she found dry cloth heated by warm skin. She couldn't get close enough, touch enough of him.

Cole must have felt the same. He fumbled with the buttons of her coat, making a low sound of frustration when they wouldn't part fast enough to suit him. Using both hands he ripped it open, popping buttons off into the mud. Then his hands were all over her, too—stomach, waist, breasts.

It was a rough wooing. It made her wild.

He ran his hands up her back, then down to her butt, cupping her and pulling her up against him. But he was too tall. He rubbed against her stomach through their clothes—then, when she went up on tiptoe, rubbed lower.

But not low enough. Not quite.

When he pulled her down, she sank with him to the ground, shielded by trees and rain and the gathering darkness. If the earth below her was cold, the rain had made it giving, and the air was sweet with the scents of sage and rain and wet earth.

He held himself up on his hands, his legs tangled with hers and his pelvis pressing against hers. She moaned, the sound lost in the rush of the rain. He brought his face close to hers—then, instead of kissing her, he rubbed his cheek against hers, a sandpaper tenderness that made her breath hitch.

"Dixie," he breathed against her cheek. Just that. Just her name. For a moment they lay tight and close in the damp and the darkness, unmoving. Holding on to each other.

But her body's urgency wouldn't be denied. Her hips lifted, rolled against him. He responded by raising up to gather the skirt of her dress with one hand, then slid his hand between her legs. She jolted at the first touch.

"Now?" he asked. "Now, Dixie?"

"Yes." She pushed up with her feet, lifting her hips, and he yanked down her panties and tossed them away. When she reached for the zipper on his slacks, his hand was already there. Together they freed him. Then he was cupping her bottom with his hands and pushing inside.

The heat and length of him were perfect. But it had been a long time for her, long enough for the muscles to be tight, resistant. She moaned with frustration, in no mood for slow and easy, and thrust up hard. And he filled her.

He gasped out something, but the words were lost in the storms, inner and outer. Slowly he withdrew, and just as slowly returned. Her world narrowed to *now*—to this moment when the ground was soft and chill against her back, and the rain fell in a liquid rush on leaves, on earth and puddles, as Cole slid slowly back inside her.

She gripped his hips and held him there, held him tight against her, wanting to hold on to the moment. To somehow stop time and stay here, like this, with him.

But time and their bodies defeated her. The moment slipped away in a flood of urgency as he began to move—faster, harder, smacking himself into her with thrusts that shoved her into the ground, winding her tighter and tighter until she cried out, her nails digging into arms rigid with tension, her body bucking. She heard him call out as her mind spiraled off into a place where *now* was white and endless.

Slowly her thoughts reassembled. There was a stone digging into her left buttock. Cole lay on top of her, his chest heaving. He was heavy. Her skirt was up around her waist. She was wet, muddy and cold.

And smiling. A few seconds later, she was giggling.

He groaned and propped himself up on his elbows, frowning down at her. "What?"

In answer, she dug her fingers into a particularly squelchy spot of mud on her right side and painted a big stripe down his nose.

He didn't move, didn't speak. Then he snorted—and then he rolled off her onto the cold, wet ground, laughing. "I can't believe I…we…"

"In the mud!" Giggles wound up into laughter. "Both of us, in the mud!"

"Oh, yeah." He was laughing hard now, holding his stomach. "Such romance, such… I swept you off your feet, didn't I?"

"Right off them, and plopped me down in the mud." She began to sing "Some Enchanted Evening" seriously off-key, the words interrupted by giggles.

Cole hummed along, propped up on one elbow, then bent over and kissed her. "I guess this proves I can get down and dirty."

That sent her off into renewed laughter, more than the small joke warranted. But she felt so *good*.

"Come on, my muddy partner in lust." He rolled to his feet, zipped his pants and held out a hand. "Let's get you inside and warmed up."

"My panties," she said, taking his hand and letting him pull her up. "And my shoe," she added when she noticed she was lopsided.

Fortunately, the shoe wasn't far. Cole presented it to her with a bow. But it was almost completely dark now, though the rain had slowed to a drizzle. "I'm afraid the panties are lost in action," he said.

"We have to find them," she insisted, slipping the wet shoe back on. Yuck. It was cold. "Or someone else will."

"No one will know who they belonged to."

"Oh, now I feel better." But when she looked around she knew he was right. She'd never find them in the dark. She slid an arm around his waist, he put his arm around her shoulders, and they started back. "I'm going to have to buy Merry a new raincoat. This one's ruined."

"You're wearing my sister's coat?" he asked, appalled. "I made love to you on my sister's coat?"

She started giggling again.

They made it to the carriage house unobserved— or so she hoped. Surely no one else was idiotic enough to be out at night in this weather. There they left a trail of clothes on their way to the bathroom, where a warm shower chased away the goose bumps.

Steam, proximity and soap-slick skin had an inevitable effect. But this time they could linger over kisses, touch lightly here, tease a little there. She rediscovered the sensitive spot on his throat, and he remembered the place at the end of her spine where a light stroking made her crazy.

Not that he would indulge her, not until they were both dry and horizontal on a clean, warm bed. She had to admit he had a point—but she also had to pay him back for making her wait.

She knew just how to do that. With hands and lips and tongue she explained payback to him, and she showed no mercy.

Neither did he.

Dixie's bedroom was in the loft, and she'd left the curtains open. By the time she lay lax and limp with sweat cooling on her skin, the sky had cleared. The room was awash in moonlight. The only sound was the quiet *tick-tick-tick* of her windup travel clock…and, from downstairs, a faint crunching as Hulk helped himself to a late-night snack.

Hulk…deserted by someone, claimed by her. Just as Cole had rescued an abandoned Tilly.

We're so alike in some ways, so different in others, she thought, snuggling her head a little more cozily into his shoulder. His eyes were closed, but the half smile on his lips said he wasn't sleeping. Just drifting.

She ran her fingers over his chest, loving his skin, his ribs, the small patch of hair right over his heart. Marveling at the fact that she was lying in Cole's arms once more…and in love once more.

Or still? *Who could say?* she thought drowsily, her eyelids heavy. Life sure was strange.

Maybe there had been a little seed, deep in her heart, left behind by the time when she'd loved him before. A seed that had sprouted the day she saw him again, and flourished…nourished in part, she admitted, by lust. Not much doubt that the seed had burst into full, unmistakable bloom when they rolled around in the mud together.

Partners in lust, she thought, and smiled. She and Cole hadn't truly been friends before. They'd been too young—afraid of being hurt, maybe, but also afraid of being fools. Afraid to trust. They'd loved, but with one foot out the door, ready for the moment when the other failed them.

The passion was still there, but this time there was also friendship. A surprising and very dear friendship. This time, they had a chance…if they were patient with each other, willing to be foolish….

Cole's hand, stroking her hair, brought her back from a doze. Her eyelids lifted partway. "Mmm," she said, to encourage him.

"You still with me?"

"Let's see." She wiggled a foot, fluttered the fingers of one hand. "All the parts seem to be in place, but I've misplaced my bones. Think overcooked spaghetti. Melted butter. Jell-O."

"You sound hungry." He was amused, but there was an ounce of hesitation in his next words. "But happy."

"I am." Her eyes were drifting shut again. "Very happy. I'm going to marry you."

Her eyes popped open. She couldn't believe she'd said that.

Neither could Cole, judging by the way he jolted. "What the...you're joking, right?"

She'd never been more serious in her life. But if she said that, Cole would be back in his clothes and out the door in under two minutes. So she mustered a decent chuckle. "How about another bet? If I get you to propose, you have to be my sex slave for a month."

He relaxed and tugged at a strand of her hair. "And if I don't, you're my sex slave? That's an offer I can't refuse. Be prepared to pay up."

His obvious relief hurt. But she had an uphill road to climb, and she knew it. She'd left Cole once. That was the one unforgivable sin in his book. He had a tendency to shove people who left him into a mental box and leave them there, where they couldn't hurt him again.

But as she'd told him, the problem with boxes was that their lids could pop off. Dixie meant to do anything and everything she could to break out of whatever mental compartment Cole had shoved her in. So she teased him, keeping things light, until he dozed off.

Then she plotted.

Words weren't going to win Cole. Eleven years ago she'd told him she loved him, and she'd left him anyway. If you want to convince a man of something, she decided, you needed to use man-language. And man-language means actions, not words.

How would a man go about convincing a woman he was serious?

Dixie smiled, snuggled close to the man sleeping beside her, and laid her plans.

Nine

The sun was shining brightly through Cole's office window three days later as he punched in a number he'd gotten from a friend. He glanced at his watch as a phone rang on the other end. He needed to get this taken care of before Dixie showed up. She was taking him to lunch today, and he didn't want her to know about...

"Hampstead Investigations," a female voice said in his ear.

"My name is Cole Ashton. I'd like to speak with Mr. Hampstead about an investigation."

"I'd be happy to make an appointment for you, sir."

"I prefer to speak with Mr. Hampstead first."

"Very well. He's on another line. Can you hold for a moment?"

Cole agreed, tapping his fingers on the desk. He caught sight of the orchid sitting on the corner of his desk and his lips curved unwillingly. It looked right there somehow.

Dixie had had it delivered the day after they made love. The next day she'd given him a box of chocolate-covered pecans, and yesterday she'd brought him a small, exquisitely wrapped box. That turned out to be cuff links—handmade, with turquoise set in heavy silver. They'd looked alarmingly expensive, but when he'd protested she'd laughed and said a friend of hers made them.

It was almost as if she was courting him.

Get real, he told himself, glancing at his watch again. This was Dixie. She was playing at role reversal and enjoying the game, that was all.

A pleasant tenor came on the line. "This is Frank Hampstead, Mr. Ashton. How may I help you?"

"I've a confidential family matter I need investigated. I prefer not to drive down to the city right now to see you in person." Cole felt foolish enough about consulting a private investigator. He didn't want to feel foolish in person. "I'm hoping we can arrange things over the phone."

"I generally insist on meeting my clients, sir. You'd be amazed at what some people will do— using a fake name, for example, which complicates the billing process considerably."

"Abe said you'd feel that way." The friend Cole

named was an attorney with a great many connections in this part of the state.

A spark of interest entered the other man's voice. "Abe Rosenberg?"

"Yes, I got your name from him. He suggested you could call him to establish my bona fides."

Hampstead put Cole on hold again while he called Abe. Cole drummed his fingers and looked at the orchid sitting there so bright and exotic.

He wasn't going to take her seriously. That's where he'd gone wrong before, thinking Dixie meant the love words she'd spoken. He supposed she had, at the time. But for Dixie, *I love you* didn't mean *I want to be with you forever.*

He'd enjoy her, enjoy their affair and keep his heart out of it. When it ended, he'd wish her well…and maybe they could remain friends. He found that he really wanted that. If ending their affair meant losing her altogether again…

"Sorry to keep you waiting, Mr. Ashton," Hampstead said. "Tell me about this family matter you need information about. Confidentiality," he added, "is a given."

"It's complicated." Cole paused. He hated discussing his father, but this was necessary. Briefly he explained about the recent advent of Grant "Ashton" into their lives. "I've no real reason to doubt him," Cole finished. "But no reason to believe him, either, and I need to know the truth. The marriage license he showed us doesn't prove anything. I don't know how one goes about obtaining a fraudulent marriage license, but it must be possible."

"And there is potentially a great deal of money involved," Hampstead agreed. "You're wise to be cautious."

As far as Cole was concerned, if Grant wanted to try to swindle Spencer Ashton out of some part of his fortune, more power to him. Cole wouldn't allow his family to be hurt by the man, however. "I don't want anyone to know I'm having him investigated. My family has accepted Grant. They'd be upset if they knew I'd sicced a private eye on him."

"No problem. I only report to my client, and there should be no need to ask questions of any of your family members."

"So is this marriage something you can prove or disprove definitely?"

"Certainly. I'll need a few more specifics from you, then we'll go over my fees."

They wrapped up the conversation and were going over the detective's rates and expenses when something tapped on Cole's window. He looked that way, puzzled.

The sky was completely clear, and he was on the second floor. He must have imagined it. "That's acceptable," he told Hampstead. "You have my number. When can I expect to hear from you?"

"Perhaps in a few days, but all sorts of things can complicate this sort of investigation. Many older records are not in computer databases. If I have to check courthouse records in person, for example, it will take longer."

Plink. Plink-plink.

"And cost more, obviously," Cole said, pushing his chair back. "Fine. Let me know when you learn something." They exchanged obligatory goodbyes, and Cole disconnected. Frowning, he got up and went to the window.

Another pebble hit it as he arrived. And below, ready to toss more missiles his way, was Dixie…on the back of his mother's horse, with his horse in tow. She wore jeans, a denim jacket with a hot pink T-shirt and a battered black cowboy hat.

Cole shook his head, grinning. God only knew where she'd gotten the hat. He opened the window and leaned out. "You don't know how to ride."

"And yet here I am, on a horse. I must have learned at some point." Her face was tilted up to him, her grin as wide-open as the day. "Come along quietly now, and no one will get hurt. You're being kidnapped."

Dixie might be all play, but she was incredibly fun to play with. He shook his head. "Uh-uh. I want to be the bad guy. You can be the marshal and arrest me."

"This is an abduction," she told him severely. "Marshals do not abduct people. Besides, I've got the black hat. I get to be the outlaw."

Cole was grinning as he took the stairs two at a time. He could faintly hear one of the girls in the tasting room giving her spiel, so he took the rear exit.

They had a bad habit of introducing him to the tourists if he walked through at the wrong time, and he didn't feel like making nice to the customers right now. He wanted to see Dixie.

"You look great," he said as he came up to her, laying a hand on her knee. "Almost as if you knew what you were doing."

"Of course I do. Riding's easy. There's no clutch to worry about."

"Thank God." Cole had vivid memories of trying to teach Dixie how to drive a standard transmission. He ran a hand over the girth. "Seems tight, but Trouble has a bad habit of holding his breath." He went to his horse, who was trying to snatch a bite of grass.

"Don't you trust me to get it right?" she demanded.

"Did you saddle them?" The girth was fine.

She flashed a dimple at him. "No."

He laughed. "I didn't think so."

"So I'm not a cowgirl. I did make the picnic food. We've got a beef and sausage tart, marinated baby veggies and—hey!"

Tilly rounded the front corner of the building at a dead run. Trouble sidestepped, throwing his head back. Cole grabbed for the reins. "Damn that cat of yours! Let go before he pulls you off!"

But it wasn't Dixie's cat in pursuit this time. It was a Doberman.

Tilly made for Cole, who was trying to keep Trouble from trampling both of them. Cole hollered at the

Doberman, hoping to scare him off—which scared Tilly, who yelped and retreated.

The Doberman slowed but was growling, hackles raised, looking as if he meant to rip out Tilly's throat. Caroline's mare was normally a placid creature, but this was too much for her. She reared. Dixie slid off just as the Doberman hurled himself at Tilly.

And Hulk launched himself at the Doberman.

The cat seemed to have come out of nowhere. He landed on the dog's shoulders and rode him like a bronc buster—only with claws instead of a saddle for purchase. They served him well. The Doberman yelped and yelped again as he began running in circles.

Trouble was panicked, trying to get away. Cole didn't dare let go, but he wanted desperately to check on Dixie, who was sitting up, cradling her arm. "Are you all right?" he called.

A man came around the corner—large, red faced and yelling. "Dammit, Mustard, I said—hey! Get your cat off my dog!"

Cole swung toward him. "You're the owner of this animal?"

"Damn right I am, and if he's hurt, you'll be hearing from me!"

Hulk made his own dismount, a graceful leap to the ground followed by a bounce up to a high windowsill. Which was probably where he'd come from in the first place. The Doberman beat a quick retreat to his owner, tail between his legs.

Cole, still gripping Trouble's reins, advanced on the red-faced man, who was checking his trembling dog for wounds. "That dog," he said softly, "very nearly caused a disaster. What is your name, sir?"

"Ralph Endicott. But you can't go blaming it all on my poor Mustard. He's bleeding, dammit!"

Cole glanced down. The wounds weren't serious, but puncture wounds did need to be treated properly. "Then you'll take him to a vet."

"Which *you* are going to pay for! That stupid mutt running around loose caused all this. Mustard wouldn't have gotten away from me if—"

"My name," Cole interrupted, his voice very soft and very cold, "is Cole Ashton. My dog is allowed to roam the grounds of my winery and vineyard. Yours is not. I require the name of your insurance company. And your lawyer, if you have one."

The color drained from the man's face. "Insurance? Lawyer? Now, see here, there's no need for all that."

"There damn sure is!" Dixie marched up, face glowing with wrath. "Your failure to control your animal is negligent, possibly criminal! I've sprained my wrist! I can't paint with a sprained wrist. Do you know how much this delay is going to cost Louret? My time alone is worth several thousand, and if this messes up their ad schedule, the television time already purchased will run to—hey, come back here!"

But the man was in full flight, one hand gripping

his dog's collar as he hurried back around the building, heading for the parking lot, and escape.

"You'd better take care of your dog!" Dixie hollered after him.

That night, Cole and Dixie lay in a sweaty heap in the bed at the carriage house, talking about Tilly's adventure. Dixie's sprained wrist had forced them to be inventive in their lovemaking. The results had been memorable.

"I *ought* to have sued that man," she grumbled. "This wrist is going to put me behind."

Cole was just glad a sprained wrist was all the hurt she'd taken. When he'd seen her go sailing off the mare's back... "You frightened him badly enough already," he said soothingly.

"I was just following your lead. Did you see the way the blood drained from his face when you mentioned lawyers?"

"Some people only pay attention when money's involved." Like his father. Cole turned the subject. "Tilly's change of heart is downright spooky."

Dixie chuckled. "You think *you're* spooked. Hulk really doesn't know how to act."

Ever since Hulk rescued Tilly from the Doberman, the dog had been following the cat with big, liquid, adoring eyes.

Cole shook his head. "I never saw a cat take on a big dog that way. Pretty smart, getting on his back where the dog couldn't get to him."

"That part's instinct. Usually they only do it if

they're cornered, though. I guess Hulk didn't want anyone else messing with his dog."

Cole snorted. "He thought the Doberman was coming after him."

"Cynic." She yawned and snuggled closer.

He ran his hand down her hair. He loved having her close enough to pet this way. "There's an art deco exhibition in Frisco this weekend. I hoped you could go with me."

"Wish I could," she said sleepily. "Weekends I stay with Aunt Jody."

For some reason that surprised Cole. She'd moved back to help take care of her aunt, so of course she'd spend time there. Yet somehow he hadn't thought of her giving up every weekend…that's where she'd been last weekend, he realized. When he'd thought she was out playing with her current boyfriend.

He grimaced. His assumptions obviously needed adjusting. "Um…she needs round-the-clock care?"

"She can't be left alone. Mom stays with her on weekdays—she's retired now, and living with her fiancé, so she can do that. We've got a home health aide who stays with her at night during the week."

That would add up fast. As delicately as possible he asked, "Is money an issue?"

"Right now we're managing okay. Aunt Jody had accumulated a pretty good nest egg for retirement, and her insurance covers most of the medical stuff. Not long-term care, though."

"I'll go with you this weekend and help." The offer slipped out unplanned, which made him uneasy. He wasn't used to making impulsive decisions. But it was the right thing to do…wasn't it?

Dixie lifted her head, then propped herself up with one arm to study his face. "Are you sure? It's a lot like taking care of a child. A large, sometimes angry child."

"I'm sure." Of course it was the right thing to do. It was the sort of thing you did for a friend, after all. He wasn't making any kind of commitment, just giving up a weekend. Big deal.

Her slow smile dawned. "Thanks, then," she said, and kissed him lightly on the lips.

Usually Aunt Jody went to bed early, in part because of her medication, but she'd been delighted to have a man around. By the time Dixie washed up in the upstairs bathroom and headed down the hall to the guest room where she and Cole were sleeping, she was exhausted.

Cole had been wonderful with Aunt Jody. When she'd come downstairs for dinner with lipstick smeared in fat circles on her cheeks in honor of his visit, he'd flirted with her gently.

Dixie had had to leave the room to cry. Jody had always been immaculate about her appearance. Elegant.

"Sorry I ducked out on you earlier," she said as she padded up to the bed.

"I tagged along to help, not to issue demerits. You're doing enough of that yourself." He held the covers up invitingly, and she climbed in beside him.

"You think you aren't supposed to have feelings about what's happening to your aunt?"

"Mama would have just smiled. It doesn't get to her like it does me." Dixie sighed and nestled close. "It's not that she doesn't care. She does, deeply. She just handles it better."

Dixie had always loved her mother…but, she admitted, she hadn't always respected her. Helen had depended on men for so much, and they'd let her down, over and over. Even Dixie's father had let her down by dying.

Years ago, Dixie had decided she wanted to be like her aunt, bold and independent, not like her mother. She was being forced to see them both in a new light. And herself.

"Your mom handles it differently than you," Cole said. "Different isn't better. Maybe it doesn't hurt her as much to see Jody being childish because she remembers her being a child. You don't. The only Jody you knew was the adult."

"Why does she have to lose that?" Dixie burst out. "She built the person she was, year by year, and now it's all being taken away!"

"I don't know, sugar." He stroked her hair. "I don't know."

Dixie was silent a few moments. "I get scared. It could happen to me."

"To any of us. And it is scary."

Cole continued stroking, and it helped. He'd helped all weekend, just by being there. He'd offered to come here with her, and that meant so much…too much? The quick spurt of fear made her bite her lip. She was relying on him too much, wanting him to be there for her, like this, from now on. That wasn't healthy...

No, she told herself. Hadn't she learned anything? She was afraid of relying on others, yes. And maybe she had reason. But pure independence didn't exist. People had to help others sometimes, but being willing to help wasn't enough. Sometimes you had to be willing to accept help, and that was a lot harder.

For her, anyway. But watching her aunt had shown her that pure self-sufficiency was an illusion.

Her eyes began to drift shut. "Sorry," she murmured. "I'm really tired."

"Then sleep. You're not my personal houri," he said, an edge to his voice. "I'll survive not having sex for one night."

That stung, mostly because there was some truth in his assumption that she felt obliged to offer sex. She didn't like seeing that about herself.

Eleven years ago, she'd believed he was mainly interested in her because of the sex, yet he'd been ready to propose. And she hadn't had a clue...his fault, in part. He'd pulled back emotionally. But she'd screwed up, too. She'd begun to depend on him, and that had scared her even more than losing him. Leaving him had been incredibly painful, yet easier than staying and facing her fears.

Not this time, she promised herself as her eyes closed. She wouldn't run away again.

Cole watched the woman sleeping in his arms. In the moon-washed darkness he could see the way sleep erased the troubles from her face. He thought he could even make out a few of the pale freckles on her nose.

Why was she so hard on herself? All weekend he'd seen a woman who found the strength to laugh with Cole at some of her aunt's absurdities, such as her conviction that they had a king, not a governor, who lived in a castle in Hollywood. Dixie had been endlessly patient, letting the older woman tell the same story again and again, acting just as interested the fifth time as the first.

At one point Jody had grown angry because Dixie wouldn't let her slice the tomatoes. She'd kicked her niece. Dixie had told her firmly that kicking wasn't allowed and gone on fixing supper.

Cole had distracted Jody at that point, but how many times had Dixie had to deal with that sort of thing when no one was around to help? And all Dixie could think about was how much better she ought to be handling things.

Had she been like this before, and he'd failed to notice? Because this wasn't the flighty, inconstant woman he'd remembered…that he'd been determined to remember, he thought with a strange ache beneath his breastbone. This was a woman who would stick by a man…if she truly loved him.

Apparently she hadn't loved Cole enough.

That was past, he told himself fiercely. They were

lovers again, but this time they weren't in love. At least, she wasn't.

Cole swallowed. He'd come close, painfully close, to falling for her all over again. He had to pull back. He didn't want this affair to end with her out of his life completely—because it would end. She'd left him before, and she would leave him again.

Not because she was lacking. Because he was.

But she wanted him. He knew that very surely. And he would use it.

Ten

Cole was pulling back. Just as he had before.

"I'm still not sure about leaving those two alone together," he said darkly as he signaled for the turn.

"Relax. Hulk has decided he likes having a groupie."

"More like an acolyte. Your cat has stolen my dog."

Dixie chuckled. "He's never had a dog of his own before. I didn't know he wanted one."

She was imagining things, she told herself. Cole liked to keep things light and friendly, yes, but that was no change. Just because he hadn't spent every one of the past five nights with her didn't mean he'd lost interest. They were on the way to his cabin now, weren't they? And he certainly hadn't looked disinterested when he invited her. He'd promised her a tour, dinner and a fire in the fireplace, and had asked her to wear her blue sundress, the one with the full skirt and buttons all the way down. He had designs on her buttons, he'd said.

She had to be patient. Just because he wasn't tumbling back into love as fast as she had didn't mean he wouldn't fall eventually. It would take time, that's all. Trust wouldn't come easily for him.

"You had your suitcase out when I picked you up," Cole said casually. "You aren't leaving yet, are you?"

"Hmm?" Dixie dragged her attention back. "No, not for another week or so. My wrist has delayed things. Didn't your mom tell you?"

"Tell me what?"

"She asked Grant to stay awhile. He's going to move into the carriage house, so I'm moving to your old room in the big house. We'd have to make other arrangements soon anyway, wouldn't we?" she added when he didn't respond. "I'll be through with all the preliminary work soon."

"And then?" he asked in an even voice.

"I'll do the paintings at my studio." Trying not to sound insecure she added, "I'm assuming you're interested in more than a couple of weeks together."

He hesitated a moment. "I'm up for a longer run if you are."

It wasn't the kind of response designed to lift her heart. Anxiety twisted in her gut, but she kept her voice dry. "Try not to overdo the hearts and flowers. You'll embarrass me."

In answer he reached out and took her hand. It helped...some.

They reached the cabin at dusk. Dixie was thinking of the other time she'd been here, without going inside. Maybe Cole was, too. He didn't say much, just opened the door, turned on the light and gestured for her to go inside.

It was not what she'd expected. "But this is fabulous!" she said, turning in a slow circle.

"Thought I'd screwed it up when I said I did the work myself, didn't you?"

"Partly." She slanted him a mischievous glance. "And partly I thought you'd go for something safer, more traditional. This looks as if an upscale designer planned it."

"Don't insult me." But he looked pleased. "I didn't do it all myself—I needed the experts to replace a load-bearing wall with those wooden pillars, and remove part of the top floor over the living area."

The entire downstairs, save for the bathroom in one corner, was one big room, with half of it two stories high. The stone fireplace was original, he said, but he'd put in the plank floors himself. He'd also replaced the Sheetrock and applied the Venetian plaster. It was a warm terra-cotta with golden undertones. "I'm impressed. I think you've invented a new style—European rustic."

"I haven't done much to the kitchen, I'm afraid."

"I'd sort of guessed that," she said dryly, looking at an avocado-green stove, a refrigerator that belonged in a museum and the single counter covered in worn Formica. "Did you ever learn how to cook?"

"Sure. I can scramble eggs with the best of them."

"If I didn't know we'd brought dinner with us, I'd be worried."

They ate on a thick, faded Oriental carpet in front of the fire—enchiladas from one of Napa's best Mexican restaurants, followed by strawberries dipped in chocolate.

And wine, of course. A rich merlot from Louret's vineyards with dinner, and French champagne with dessert. "This did not come from your winery," she pointed out.

"Nope. But I've a fondness for bubbles." He topped off her glass—again.

"Are you trying to get me drunk?" Dixie asked, amused. She sipped. "You must be hoping to have your way with me."

"You know, I believe I am."

None of the lights were on. There was just the fire to warm his skin with its orange glow, and in the dimness, Cole's eyes looked very dark, his smile secretive. "You've been having fun with your courting games. My turn now." He reached forward and gently removed the glass he'd just filled. "I think we'll get started. We're doing things my way tonight, Dixie."

Something in his voice tugged at her belly. "I can handle that."

"Can you?" He leaned in and kissed her softly, lingering over it. "You like games," he murmured against her lips.

"Mmm-hmm." She drew a line along his bottom lip with her tongue.

"And you like being in charge." He pulled back slightly, smiling. "In control."

"Sometimes." She threaded a hand into his hair to bring his mouth back.

"Uh-uh." He shook his head, still smiling…not letting her have the kiss she wanted. "We're playing a different game tonight. And you aren't in charge."

Her heartbeat kicked up. She raised one eyebrow. "No?"

"No." He reached into the basket that had held their dinner and pulled out a long red scarf. He played with it, pulling it through his hands like a silky snake. "You trust me, don't you?"

"Of course." But her mouth was dry.

"Good. Hold out your hands."

She hesitated, eyeing that scarf. "What kind of game did you have in mind?"

He just smiled. And waited.

After a moment she shrugged. "In for a penny," she said, and held out her hands.

He looped the scarf around them and tied it. The silk was cool against her skin…which was probably two degrees hotter than it had been a minute ago. "Bondage. I've never…" Her laugh came out nervous. "What do I do now?"

"Nothing." He leaned in again and kissed her

lightly, brushing his fingertips along her throat, light as a butterfly kiss. "I do it all. You aren't in control tonight, Dixie."

"I don't think I'm good at that."

"This isn't about being good. Or being good at something." He reached for her buttons. "I do like this dress," he murmured, and slid the first button loose. Then the next.

He worked slowly, button by button, all the way down. She sat there with her hands bound in silk and watched him looking at what he revealed. His heavy eyelids lifted slightly to pass her a smile when he finished. Then he parted the dress.

She wasn't wearing a bra. The way her hands were tied snugged her arms into her breasts, squeezing them together. Her breath was coming faster. "You like?" she asked, her voice husky.

"Oh, yeah." This time when he leaned close, he bent. He laved one areola slowly with his tongue, then flicked it over the nipple. She squirmed. "Hold still," he told her, and put his mouth on her other nipple, sucking lightly. "There." He sat back. "I like the way they look, wet and shiny from my mouth."

She liked the look on his face. But he was going too slowly, and she wanted to touch him. "I'm getting a little overheated."

He cocked an eyebrow at her. "The fire too hot?"

"Something is."

"Maybe you're overdressed for the occasion."

"We could take off the scarf."

He shook his head. "My game," he said softly, and

drifted his fingertips down the slopes of both breasts to their tips. He took them between his fingers and squeezed rhythmically. "But we can make you a little more comfortable. Why don't you lie down?"

He was playing with her mind as well as her breasts. And winning. The ache between her legs pulsed along with his fingers. "I…" *Am finding it hard to breathe.* "You'll have to let go first. And my hands…lying down is awkward without hands."

"Oh," he said, as if surprised. "Of course. I'll help you." And at last he looked at her face again—and in his eyes was pure heat. When he leaned close and took her mouth this time, he wasn't slow and careful.

She kissed him back, half-frantic with the need to touch, yet it was incredibly erotic to be able to touch him only with her lips, her tongue. She felt his hands at her shoulders, lowering her to the floor.

But he didn't follow her down and cover her with his body the way she craved. When he pulled away, she cried out in frustration.

"Easy," he said soothingly, stroking her legs, pushing the dress completely apart so that it puddled on the floor on either side of her. "Easy," he told her again, and put his mouth on her, right through her panties.

She jolted, so aroused that the damp warmth almost immediately brought her to the edge.

Then he stopped.

"I'm going to…" she sputtered, but couldn't think of the right threat. Maybe because she couldn't think, period. "Dammit, Cole!"

"You're not used to this. You aren't in control at all. I am." He tugged on her panties, pulling them down an inch at a time.

She narrowed her eyes. "You're enjoying this too much."

Briefly his grin flashed. "Define 'too much.' I am for damn sure enjoying myself."

That glimpse of his grin relaxed her, reminding her that this was a game. But she was finding it harder and harder to play. "I'm not sure I like feeling this vulnerable."

He tossed her panties aside. "How does this feel? Is it exciting?"

He put one finger inside her—and yes, it was exciting. Beyond exciting. She couldn't keep from moving. Two fingers… "Cole."

"Soon, sweetheart," he crooned. "Let me play a little more." Three fingers, in and out, the rhythm driving her crazy. Then his thumb pressed lightly on her, and she exploded.

Aftershocks pinged through her. She lay motionless, her eyes closed, trying to catch her breath, her muscles wasted…and she ached. Ached fiercely. After a moment she felt him, smooth and blunt, probing at her entrance, and lifted heavy eyelids. He'd scrambled out of his clothes while her eyes were closed, and at last was as naked as she.

"The scarf," she whispered, holding up her bound hands. "Take it off." She needed to be able to touch as well as be touched. Needed more than pleasure.

He paused. The arms he propped himself up with

were so rigid they shook. There was no play left in his eyes, only hunger and something akin to desperation.

He shoved inside. His face spasmed, and he groaned. And then, with shaky hands, he untied the scarf.

She gasped with relief and reached for him, and they made the last part of the journey together. It was a quick, rough climb, and if her second climax didn't hit with the force of the first, this one satisfied.

And afterward, with his weight heavy and limp on top of her, she lay there for a long while in the dying firelight, stroking him. Feeling the need to soothe him. As if he were the one who'd been pushed to the limit and beyond.

And she didn't know why. She didn't understand at all.

Eleven

Sweat rolled down Cole's forehead, stinging his eyes, as his feet thudded on the path near his cabin. He'd forgotten the sweatband—had pulled on his shorts and a T-shirt, shoved his feet into his running shoes and taken off.

The morning was barely broken, the sun a sliver at the horizon. The air was chilly—or had been, before he started running.

Too late echoed in his head with every footfall. He pushed himself a little faster.

It was amazing what a fool he'd been, thinking he could just enjoy Dixie. Thinking love was a decision, or something he could avoid, like stepping out of the way of a speeding car. Nope, no thanks, don't want to get hit today.

Too late.

Or that love could be made into play. That's all he'd meant by that game with the scarf—some sexy game. With, maybe, a whiff of the need to keep her interested, make her want to continue the affair.

Somewhere along the line it had taken a serious turn. He'd wanted her tied and bound to him. Forever.

Too late.

This morning he'd woken up reaching for her. She hadn't been there, of course. He'd taken her back to The Vines last night—a move born of panic, he admitted. She'd be sleeping now, sleeping in the room he'd moved out of years ago.

Too late, he thought, his feet dragging to a stop. He stood with his head down, his hands on his thighs, dragging in air. Maybe it had been too late from the moment she walked into his office again after an eleven-year absence.

He was in love with Dixie. Desperately in love. He was running because that's what he wanted to do—run away from the feeling. From her. It was impossible, of course. He couldn't escape what he felt. Not the love. Not the fear, either.

Or maybe he could—the fear, anyway. If he left her.

Cole had been terrified of going to the dentist as a child. When he was ten, he'd realized that the fear was as bad as the event, maybe worse. He hadn't conquered it, but he had stopped putting it off. It would happen whether he delayed or not, so why wait, dragging out the fear?

But dental visits truly couldn't be avoided. Was losing Dixie just as inevitable?

He'd been telling himself he knew she would leave. Maybe not for months, but eventually she would go. But now, faced with the prospect of living with the fear of losing her or walking away himself, he discovered a stubborn core of hope.

There were the gifts she'd given him, the orchid and chocolates, the cufflinks. Just yesterday she'd given him a goofy card, telling him sternly, "Take note. Women *love* to get cards. You get extra points for a blank card that you write in yourself."

He'd told himself they were part of the game for her, but they'd gotten to him underneath, where words don't reach.

There was the way they laughed together, too, and the sheer comfort he felt with her sometimes. And sometimes, when she was looking at him, her face seemed to glow—not with the blazing heat of desire, but a gentler warmth, like a welcoming candle. Was that just friendship? And when she'd reached for him last night as he entered her...that had felt very like love.

If only he could know, one way or the other!

Cole ran his forearm over his forehead, wiping off the sweat that was chilling him as it dried. He'd better keep moving. He'd stiffen up if he just stood here.

Slowly he started back to the cabin. He could ask her what she felt for him. That was as logical as it was terrifying. But what would it prove? Even if she said she was passionately in love, could he believe her? She'd spoken of love before. It hadn't kept her from leaving.

He had to be sure of her. One way or the other, he had to know.

Moving faster now, he laid his plans.

"Look, I'm sorry," Cole said, rubbing the back of his neck with the hand that wasn't holding the phone. "This came up unexpectedly, and I can't get out of it."

Silence.

This wasn't part of his plan. He'd put off seeing her for two days, citing work—he'd been spending a lot of time with her, he'd said, and had to catch up. It was halfway true, but the real reason was that he needed to see if she'd take off.

Having a genuine business emergency hadn't been part of his plan. "I'll make it up to you for canceling tonight. We'll go out Friday. Maybe to that new club—"

"I'll be at my aunt's on Friday night."

Right. "Okay, Thursday. We'll do whatever you want."

More silence, then: "Are you getting that déjà vu feeling? I used to hear that a lot. Or maybe you aren't feeling anything at all. That would be safer, wouldn't it?"

"Dammit, Dixie, I didn't conjure this guy out of thin air. He's the rep for a major distributor, and if he wants to talk about carrying our new chardonnay, I'm for damn sure going to talk to him. He's only in town for this one day."

"And no one else can handle this?"

"Lucas is down with a stomach bug. Mercedes and Jillian don't know enough about the production end, or where else we're committed. And Eli wouldn't know what kind of volume discount to agree to. Besides, he's lousy at this sort of thing."

"You're doing it again. Hiding behind work, finding excuses to pull back."

"Don't be childish," he snapped. "I can't dance attendance on you every minute."

The sudden dial tone in his ear made him wince. *Way to go, Ashton.* But it was the thickness he'd heard in her voice that haunted him as he got ready for his meeting. It had sounded a lot like tears.

"Dixie?" Mercedes paused in the doorway. "What's wrong?"

"Nothing." Furious at being caught crying, she wiped away the evidence.

"Right," Merry said dryly, coming into Dixie's room—the one that used to be Cole's. "I know. You're feeling sentimental because it's National Oatmeal Month."

"Always gets to me." Dixie sniffed. "National Opposites Day is coming up, too."

"And Ben Franklin's birthday. Another big occasion."

This was a game they'd played back in college, when any excuse to shop, eat chocolate or sleep in late was a good excuse. Congress was always making special days that no one paid any attention to,

Dixie had told Merry. It was their solemn duty to see that no occasion went unobserved.

"Is it National Hugging Day yet?" Dixie's smile was a tad watery, but she did feel better.

"Close enough." Merry honored the almost-occasion by giving Dixie a hug. "So what's up? Your work going okay?"

Dixie flopped her hand in a so-so gesture. In fact, work was going fine—so well that she was dragging out the last sketches so she'd have an excuse to stay at The Vines a little longer.

Merry sat on the bed beside her. "Your aunt?"

"Not this time. Your brother."

"Uh-oh. I thought things were going great with you two. Tell me what's wrong. As long as it doesn't involve sex," she added hastily. "I do not want to hear about your sex life when it's my brother you're having sex with."

"Oh, no. The sexual part of our relationship makes me scream with joy, not cry."

Merry looked pained.

Dixie's grin hardly wobbled at all. "Okay, okay. No sex talk. The thing is…oh, I don't know what the thing is."

She shoved to her feet and started pacing. "He's giving me these mixed signals. I'm trying not to mention sex, but that is part of it. When we're together that way, it feels important. Like I truly matter to him. But if I so much as mention the future, he turns vague. Casual."

I'm up for a longer run if you are. She sniffed

again, but more in scorn than sorrow this time. Even if they'd been having a purely casual affair, that comment lacked grace.

"Lots of men have trouble committing," Merry offered. "It takes them longer to admit what they're feeling. You two haven't been back together very long, Dixie."

"I know, but…oh, everything I could mention sounds trivial. I haven't seen him for two days, and he just canceled our dinner tonight. That shouldn't be a big deal, and yet…it's not what he does, but the way he does it. I feel like it's happening all over again," she finished sadly. "Just like eleven years ago. I can feel his walls going up."

And she wasn't sure she could handle it. All the pep talks in the world didn't stop the hurt. Or the doubts. How could she make herself believe she could count on Cole when, for no reason she could see, he suddenly started tacking up Keep Out signs?

Merry didn't say anything for several moments. "Cole's got walls," she admitted. "Big, high, scary ones. Half the time you seem to slip in under them easier than anyone. The other half, you trigger them."

"Yeah." Dixie plopped down on the bed again. "I'm scared."

"Goes with the territory, unless you're sensible enough to be like me and just date losers. No gain, no pain, I always say."

"I've been meaning to talk to you about Craig," Dixie began.

"Uh-uh. No. Not today. You can give me advice after you get your love life straightened out."

"When I'm seventy, you mean?"

"If you're lucky."

Dixie sighed. Cole had promised they'd get together tomorrow night. Maybe she should press him for some frank talk. Or would that be pushing for too much, too soon?

Never mind. She'd think of something. "How about a girls' night out tonight?"

"Sorry." Merry carefully removed a piece of fuzz from her slacks. "Wednesdays I have supper with Jared. Used to be the three of us, but…" She shrugged. "We've kept it up since Chloe died. It seemed to help him, especially at first, to have someone to talk with about her. We've become good friends."

Dixie slid her a curious glance. Chloe had been a friend of theirs in college. She and Merry had stayed close afterward, since they lived nearby. But a standing dinner date with Chloe's widower six years after Chloe's death? That sounded like more than friendship…but then, who was she to say?

Merry was right. Dixie needed to get her own life figured out before she tried to straighten out anyone else's.

"I need to paint," she said suddenly. "Or go mess with paint, anyway."

An art therapy session might tell her what she needed to know—even if she wasn't sure she wanted to learn it.

* * *

Thursday afternoon Cole stared at the faxed report in his hand. His brain felt numb. Fuzzy. Rain beat against the office window. The only light came from his desk lamp. All else had faded into gloom with the arrival of the storm.

He shook his head. This couldn't be right. There had to be some mistake. He reached for the phone and punched in the number of the detective who'd investigated Grant Ashton.

Fifteen minutes later the numbness was gone. Rage gathered in its place, questions ping-ponged around in his head—and beneath all lay a vast bewilderment.

The detective would bill him. How was he supposed to sign the check? *Cole Ashton*...that's who he was, who he had been all his life.

He could have become Cole Sheppard when he was ten. Lucas had wanted to adopt them, but Spencer had refused to relinquish his rights. He hadn't wanted his children, but he hadn't wanted anyone else to claim them, either.

And now he'd made Cole's entire life into a lie.

Cole slammed his fist down on the desk. "Damn him!" He jerked to his feet, grabbed his jacket and headed for the door. And didn't notice that his jacket had brushed against the delicate orchid sitting on one corner of his desk, sending it crashing to the floor.

Twelve

Cole drove for hours. Drove through the rage and into bitterness. Passed from that to bewilderment and questions, many of which couldn't be answered from behind the wheel of his Suburban. But they could be listed mentally, ordered, given consideration and assigned priorities. He drove until, finally, he had to pull over at a motel and sleep before he killed himself and maybe others.

Hours later, he woke to the sound of traffic. Light streamed through the cracks between the wall and the fiberglass drapes. He was fully dressed, the bed beneath him was hard, and there was a water stain on the ceiling.

For a moment he had no idea where he was or

how he'd gotten there. Slowly memory seeped back. With it came another fact.

Today was Friday. The day that regularly arrived right after Thursday—which was when he'd promised to take Dixie out.

He groaned. Could his timing have possibly been worse?

She'd understand, he told himself as he rushed through a shower. There wasn't much hot water, but he didn't see anything with too many legs crawling around, which was a relief, given the condition of his accommodations.

Which were where, exactly? He wasn't even sure what part of the state he was in. No, wait—he dimly remembered crossing the state line shortly before he decided to pull over. He was in Nevada. Somewhere in Nevada. They'd know at the front desk.

As he scrambled into yesterday's clothes, he assured himself that once he told Dixie what he'd learned, she'd understand why everything else had been blasted clean out of his mind.

Dressed, somewhat damp and more than a little desperate, he tried to call her. But the phone by the bed didn't work, and he'd forgotten his cell phone. He'd rushed out the door without anything but his jacket and what he'd had in his pockets.

He'd run off without calling Dixie.

She was going to ask why. She probably would understand that he'd been badly shaken. She was a compassionate person. But she'd wonder why it had never once occurred to him to turn to her.

So did he.

* * *

Cole gassed up, grabbed a breakfast burrito and a large coffee, and left the tiny town of Basalt, Nevada, behind. He didn't stop again until he pulled up in front of his parents' house five endless hours later.

He'd driven longer last night, but last night he'd lacked any kind of destination. Time hadn't mattered. It did now.

Tilly rushed up to greet him as soon as he stepped out, and he was smitten by guilt. Someone would have fed her when it was obvious he'd taken off, but he must have worried everyone. Including his dog.

He took a moment to pet and reassure Tilly, then headed into the house. It was two in the afternoon, so Dixie would be working—which meant she might be anywhere. But she'd set her easel up in the lanai, so he checked there first.

No sign of her. Or anyone else, for that matter. No one seemed to be home at all.

He'd check her room anyway, just to make sure. He took the stairs two at a time.

She wasn't there, but Mercedes was. She was packing Dixie's things.

Cole stood in the doorway, frozen. Faint and far-away, he heard the echo that had haunted him on his morning run three days ago: *too late, too late, too late...*

Mercedes finished folding a pair of slacks, laid them carefully in Dixie's suitcase and straightened, scowling at him. "It's about time you showed up! Where in the world have you been?"

"I'll tell you later." He would have to. They'd all have to know. But right now his lips were numb and there wasn't enough air. He could barely get the next words out. "Where is she?"

"Gone, obviously," Mercedes snapped.

"Mercy." The childhood nickname slipped out as he crossed to her and put his hands on her shoulders. "I have to find her. I *have* to. Where did she go?"

Mercedes searched his face. Her expression softened into worry. "She didn't leave because you're a jerk. You are, but that isn't why she left."

The quick stab of anxiety made him tense. "Then why?"

"Her mother had a heart attack yesterday."

"Oh, no." Cole closed his eyes for a second. "Is she—?"

"It was a mild one, apparently. She's in the hospital now, but they say she'll be okay. But that isn't all. She called the ambulance herself when she realized what was happening. Only…" She swallowed. "She was taking care of Jody at the time. And in all the confusion, Jody wandered off."

"Oh, God." Cole thought about the storm last night. "Tell me she isn't still missing."

"I can't. She's been gone almost a full day now."

Dixie sat at the table in her aunt's kitchen with her head in her hands. The table was covered by maps—a large topographic map, a city map, a county map.

She couldn't think of anything else to do, anywhere to look that they hadn't already checked. How far could a confused sixty-year-old woman go?

The phone rang. She'd been carrying it from room to room with her, so she grabbed it immediately. "Yes?"

It was Jillian, checking in. Everyone had been so good. They'd practically shut Louret down for the day in order to look for Jody. The authorities were looking, too, of course. It just wasn't doing much good.

Everyone was looking…except Cole. Who had vanished as completely as her aunt.

His mother had told her not to worry too much about him. "He does this sometimes," she'd said gently. "When Cole has a personal snarl he needs to work through, he drives."

Dixie knew what snarl he was working on. Her. Apparently she was a huge snarl, too, since he'd not only stood her up, but had stayed gone all night. Somewhere around midnight, up at the hospital, she'd decided she'd take care of that tangle for him. If it was that hard to decide whether he even wanted to go out to dinner with her…

When the back door opened she looked up dully, expecting one of the searchers.

It was Cole.

She went hot, then cold, the fluctuation hitting as abruptly as if a switch had been thrown. For a second she wondered if she might faint, which would be too mortifying to bear. She looked away.

"No word?" he asked softly.

She shook her head and looked at the table. She'd had too little sleep, that was all. A couple hours snatched on a hard couch in the waiting room at the hospital. She didn't *need* Cole, not after he'd shown her how true all her doubts had been.

But her aunt might. There were colored buttons on the topo map, each representing a searcher or group of searchers. She cleared her throat. "If you're here to help look for Aunt Jody, fine. I'll assign you an area. If you're here for anything else, go away."

"I'll search. But I want to know how you're holding up."

"I'm fine." Her stupid, traitorous eyes chose that moment to water. "I'll be fine. This area, here, by Waters Street." She tapped the city map. "It's been searched already, but they might have missed her. Or she could have wandered back after they looked. There's a coffee shop there. It's…it was…one of her favorite…" Her voice broke as her eyes filled, and she finished in a whisper. "She might find her way there."

"Ah, hell, sweetheart." He crossed to her quickly, pulled her out of the chair and folded his arms around her.

She hit him in the chest with both fists. "Don't you call me sweetheart! Damn you, where did you—where—" But the tears were winning, her words broken apart by sobs. "I wanted you last night! I needed you, and you pulled a vanishing act!"

"I know, honey. I'm sorry. So sorry. Cry it out. You can hit me later. Hate me later."

At first she tried to break loose, but he held her too closely. Or maybe she just gave up. It felt too good to have his arms around her, his strength to lean on. So she cried.

It didn't last long. Dixie didn't understand how some people could cry for hours—when tears hit her, they hit hard and fast. And left just as fast, like a storm in the desert.

Once she was through crying, she pulled away. She didn't want to, which infuriated her. She wiped her face, sniffed, and looked around for the tissues. Crying always made her nose run.

Cole handed her the box.

"Thanks," she said, making it as cold as she could. She blew her nose.

"Have you had any sleep?"

"A little. And before you ask, I'm not going to go lie down. Later I'll have to. I don't have to yet."

He studied her face a moment. "All right. I'll tell you what happened last night, but later. How's your mom? I could take over here for a bit so you could go see her."

"She'd just send me back here. Or tell me to sleep—as if I could." Dixie sniffed one last time and tossed the tissue in the trash. "It's ridiculous! She blames herself, as if she could have timed her heart attack better!"

He nodded. "I should've known you came by that tendency honestly."

She scowled. "What are you talking about?"

"Tell me you aren't convinced you should have somehow kept this from happening. Maybe you think you should have stayed with Jody last night. You had no idea you would be needed, but you ought to have guessed. Or maybe you should have intuitively known that your mother's heart was going to act up. Or—"

"I get the point." She even felt the ghost of a smile touch her lips. "It's not my fault. I know that, and yet…" She rubbed her forehead wearily. "It's just so awful to think of Jody out there somewhere. She must be so frightened. Maybe she's hurt, or…."

"And hard to stop thinking about it. Come on," he said, taking her arm. "Sit down. Have you eaten?"

She let him steer her to a chair. "Your mother force-fed me a sandwich a couple hours ago." There. That was a real smile this time. "I don't know how she can speak so softly, be so gentle and polite and be utterly immovable at the same time."

"That's my mom." He was rummaging in the cabinets. "How about some coffee? It won't make you feel better, but you can worry more alertly."

Coffee actually sounded good. "Okay." She wasn't forgiving him. She just didn't have the energy to hate him right now. "It's in the cabinet by the sink. Make plenty," she added. "People come and go a lot."

Neither of them spoke as he prepared the pot. When it was ready, he sat down with her and his own cup and had her tell him who was searching, where they all were, what areas had already been searched.

It steadied her, reminding her that they were doing all they could.

Over the next hour one of the police officers stopped by and had a cup of coffee. He briefed them on what the official searchers were doing. The phone rang a couple of times—Mercedes called to say she was on her way back, then a telemarketer gave Dixie a chance to snarl at someone.

Cole didn't seem to be going anywhere. He seemed to have an instinct for when to speak and distract her, when to remain silent. She was pacing again when she decided she couldn't let him hang around and coddle her. "The cops took another look on Waters Street, but you could check out that gully by the supermarket."

"I'll do that." He took another sip of coffee. "Just as soon as Mercedes gets here."

She wanted him to stay. The longing was as stupid as it was selfish, when she ought to be pushing him out the door—for her own sake as well as Aunt Jody's. "I don't need to be baby-sat."

"You don't need to be alone right now, either."

She was mustering up the anger to snap at him when the phone rang again. She glanced at it and grimaced. "If that's another telemarketer—"

"I'll get it." He snaked out an arm and snagged it before she could. "Hello?"

His face told the story before he spoke. "That's wonderful. Yes…of course. We'll be right there." He put the phone down and stood, his smile wide. "She's at the newspaper office in Napa. God only knows how she got there, but she's okay. They're feeding her doughnuts. She's tired and grouchy and she doesn't want to leave," he added wryly. "She thinks she works there."

Dixie's eyes closed. Her knees all but buckled beneath the wave of relief. "She did," she managed to say. "Thirty years ago."

Thirteen

Cole drove Dixie to the newspaper offices. On the way she placed a dozen phone calls, notifying everyone who was searching that Jody had been found.

Jody had marched into the newspaper offices as if she belonged, moving so assuredly that, despite her bedraggled appearance, the receptionist hadn't stopped her. She'd stopped in the middle of the bullpen and demanded to know what they'd done with her desk. One of the reporters had realized she was the missing woman they'd been notified about. She'd settled Jody at an old typewriter so she could "get to work," and called the police.

Cole helped coax Jody into leaving work early, then soothed, flirted with and cajoled her out of a temper fit when she learned she had to stay in the hospital overnight for observation.

Jody did not like hospitals. She was somewhat mollified when she found out her sister was there, though, and fell asleep right after supper. She'd had a rough twenty-four hours. She probably would have died from exposure if she hadn't found an unlocked car last night. She'd curled up in the back seat and slept.

Her version of things, of course, was a little different. For once, the mists of Alzheimer's had some benefit—she didn't remember being lost and terrified. She believed she'd been driving to work when the rain hit, and had pulled over and gone to sleep. "Then the stupid car wouldn't start," she'd grumbled, "so I got out and walked."

God only knew how far she'd walked before she saw something that looked familiar to her shrouded mind—the newspaper office—and went inside. It was strange, Dixie thought, but some things about her aunt hadn't changed. Like her indomitable spirit. She might not have known where she was, how she got there or how to get home, but she hadn't given up.

It had been weird, going back and forth between the two hospital rooms. Dixie and her mother laughed about it, agreeing that the hospital really ought to put the sisters on the same floor to make things easier for their visitors.

Little aftershocks of fear kept pinging through Dixie when she thought about what might have happened. She wished she could find the owners of that car and thank them for not locking it. She wished…a huge yawn shut down her fuzzy thoughts.

"We're there," Cole said, pulling up in the drive-way of Jody's home.

So they were. It was ten o'clock at night after an extraordinarily long day with almost no sleep the night before. She was brain-dead with fatigue, but she did notice it when Cole got out, too.

Dixie stopped with one foot on the porch, staring at him through narrowed eyes. She ought to shake his hand, thank him and send him on his way. That would be the smart thing to do…only she was so tired. And it felt so right for him to be here.

His wry smile suggested he'd guessed some of her thoughts. "C'mon, warrior," he said, draping an arm around her shoulders and nudging her toward the door. "You can be tough tomorrow. Tonight you're staggering like a drunk woman. You need sleep."

She let him steer her into the house, then pulled free. "You're not sleeping with me," she informed him as she headed upstairs, but her voice may have lacked conviction. The yawns were hitting with every other word now.

He didn't follow her up the stairs, though, so it seemed he'd accepted the boundaries she'd set. Good, she told herself. But she felt weepy with frus-tration when she couldn't find her suitcase. Where had Merry put the stupid thing?

Never mind. She stripped and climbed into bed,

and that was all she knew for several hours…except for a few moments when she rose partway from the depths and noticed Cole's arm around her waist, his breathing steady and quiet in the darkness.

That was all right, then. She went back to sleep.

She woke at nine-ten the next day—rested, alone and confused.

For several minutes she lay quietly in bed, remembering the day before. And the night, when nothing had happened…except that it had, somehow. While she was sleeping, something had changed.

When she pushed back the covers and sat up, she smelled bacon and saw her suitcase. Had it been by the foot of the bed all along, or had Cole brought it up?

A frown pleating her forehead, she gathered some clothes and headed down the hall to the bathroom for a shower. Thirty minutes later, she went downstairs.

She wasn't surprised to find Cole still there, reading the paper. "Your mom and your aunt both spent a good night. We can pick Jody up around noon."

We? She nodded cautiously, heading for the coffeepot. "Thanks for checking on them."

"I wanted to know, too. Coffee's reasonably fresh," he added, looking back at his paper, "but the bacon's cold. Do you want some eggs?"

Her mouth twitched. His one culinary achievement. "I'm okay with bacon and toast." She padded to the pantry and took out the bread.

Neither of them spoke as Dixie put together a simple breakfast. Cole seemed entirely comfortable with both the silence and the company. Or else he was just absorbed in his newspaper.

Dixie, on the other hand, felt uncharacteristically awkward, off balance. Naturally this made his ease irritating. "Anything interesting in the news?" she asked as she brought her toast, bacon and coffee to the table.

He looked up with a slight smile. "You interested in the Dow Jones?"

"No."

"Then probably not." He went back to his paper.

She resisted the urge to snatch it out of his hands, congratulated herself on her maturity and applied herself to her meal.

He'd left the back door open. The air was fresh and surprisingly warm, the sky clear and sunny. She could hear birds talking to each other, the hum of tires on the street out front and giggles mixed with bouncing noises from next door. The kids there had a trampoline.

Cole had never liked having the TV or radio on first thing in the morning. Neither did she.

When she finished eating she carried the plate to the dishwasher, loaded it and brought the coffeepot back with her. She poured herself a second cup, then topped off Cole's. And spoke. "Put the paper down."

He looked up. After a moment he nodded, unsmiling this time, and folded the paper. "Do I get a trial, or are we going straight to the sentencing?"

"We're still in the investigation stage." She sat across from him, sipping coffee and studying him over the rim of the mug. "Why?" she asked softly. "Why did you run?"

For a long moment he looked at her, not speaking. He drummed his fingers once, then nodded. "I'll tell you what happened—now, if you like—but it had nothing to do with you. I'm hoping you'll be willing to reach a verdict without knowing more."

She shook her head, confused. "Why not just tell me?"

For a moment she glimpsed emotion, stark and ragged, in his eyes. Then he looked away. "This isn't easy for me to say, but you were right. I've been holding back from you emotionally. Making excuses to stay away. I did it on purpose. I was testing you."

Feelings rippled through her, strong and complex. "I guess I failed, then, if you had to run off."

"No." His head swung back. "I told you, that had nothing to do with you. I found out something about my father. Something…" He shook his head. "I should have come to you. It didn't occur to me, which doesn't say much for the way I handle things, but…all I can say in my defense is that I've always kept stuff about him to myself. I reacted the way I'm used to reacting. I went off to deal with it alone."

She hurt for him. "What did you learn?"

"It's big, it's important, but not as important as this." He reached across the table and took her hands in his. "Not as important as what I finally realized. I wanted you to love me, you see."

She swallowed. "Cole—"

"Let me finish." His grip tightened. "I didn't just want you to love me—I wanted you to prove it. I thought I couldn't live with the uncertainty. Then, when I came back from my driveabout, I thought you'd left me." His voice turned bleak. "That cleared things up wonderfully for me. I'd driven you away."

He was talking faster now, the words tumbling out. "All I could think was that I wanted you back. No tests, no guarantees—none of that mattered. I wanted you back. Period." He met her eyes, then one corner of his mouth kicked up. "And then, of course, I found out that your leaving didn't have a thing to do with me."

She blinked several times. She'd cried too much in the past two days. "No, it didn't. But why don't you want to tell me why you left?"

"Because," he said softly, "I wonder if you're doing the same thing I was. Testing me. Waiting for me to fail. If you need reasons to trust me, Dixie, I'll give them to you. This is not a test. But I'm hoping…" He had to stop and swallow. "I'm hoping you'll take me on faith. Because that's how I'm taking you from now on. I love you, and love means trust, not tests."

Just like that, the thing that had changed while she slept fell into clear, shining focus. Somewhere along the line she'd stopped seeing Cole. All she'd been able to see were her fears. But those fears had been phantoms, and they'd faded when real tragedy loomed…then evaporated once he was there with her.

As if she'd swallowed a year's worth of sunshine and it was rising, irresistibly making its way into every cell of her body and every corner of her mind, Dixie smiled, slow and certain. "Good. Because I'm crazy in love with you."

He let out one clear, loud crow of laughter. "Then come here, woman! What are you doing so far away?"

She was laughing, too, as he caught her up in his arms. Oh, she was caught, all right—caught for good, hopelessly entangled, tied up in knots…and set free in Cole's arms.

Epilogue

"**D**o you think your mother is ever going to forgive me?" Dixie asked, leaning forward to check her lipstick in the mirror on the back of the visor. It was nearly eight at night. They were running a little late—but it had been a busy day.

"No need," Cole said wryly. "She blames me entirely for our decision to run off to Vegas. You're in the clear."

"Well, my mother blames me for depriving her of a wedding, and thinks you hung the moon. So we're even." She flipped the visor up, smiled at the ring on her finger and glanced in the back of the suvvy.

Tilly was curled up on the back seat, sleeping. Hulk was back there, too, in his carrier—but with the carrier door open. The cat had decided that if Tilly didn't have to ride in a box, he shouldn't, either, but he wasn't ready to abandon the safety of his walls. The open carrier was a compromise.

Life was full of those. Dixie faced front again and reached for Cole's hand as they turned into the drive leading to The Vines. The big house was lit and welcoming. "You okay?" she asked softly.

He nodded without speaking. His hand was tense as he gripped hers.

So far, only his mother and stepfather knew about the detective Cole had hired, and what he'd learned. Cole had told them that afternoon, within hours of returning from Vegas. They'd agreed that the best way to present the news was in one big dose, and had arranged for everyone to be there tonight.

What Cole had to tell them would shake their worlds. No one should have to hear that kind of news secondhand.

"Everyone" included Grant now. Cole had accepted the relationship intellectually, though he had a baffled look in his eyes when he spoke of Grant. Dixie suspected he was trying too hard to feel brotherly toward a man who was still mostly a stranger.

Don't sweat it, she'd told him. It can take time for feelings to catch up. All in all, she thought he was dealing with everything remarkably well. She was proud of him.

Caroline met them at the door with a kiss and a hug for them both. Tilly and Hulk followed them in. Hulk was loudly requesting refreshments.

Caroline laughed. If there was a certain strain around her eyes, her smile was as warm as ever. "I see you brought the rest of the family with you. Everyone else is in the living room. And Hulk, if you're good I'll slip you some of the canapés. We have caviar."

"Oh, don't teach him to like that!" Dixie exclaimed. She and Caroline kept up a flow of light chatter on the way to the living room.

Cole was quiet, but no one noticed that at first. They had to hug and exclaim and chide him and Dixie for running off instead of having a proper ceremony. Dixie exchanged glances with Cole.

They'd tied the knot fast because they were sure it was right, they didn't want to wait—Cole said he was taking no chances on either of them screwing things up again—and because the family was about to be plunged into turmoil. It was not going to be a great time for an elaborate wedding.

After the first round of congratulations had run their course, Cole shifted to the center of the room. "I think Mom told you all that I had some news," he began.

"We've sort of figured it out!" Jillian said, grinning. "A sudden marriage, news to share—when am I going to be an aunt?"

Several of them laughed. Amazingly, Cole's ears turned pink. But his expression as he shook his head stilled the laughter. "Not that kind of news, I'm afraid," he said gently. "This will be upsetting. I have to start with an admission that some of you won't like. I hired a private detective to look into Grant's claims."

No, they didn't like that. It was Grant who quieted them, though. He nodded and spoke over the others. "Don't give him a hard time. It was the reasonable thing to do. Expensive," he added dryly, "but sensible."

"Thanks," Cole said, surprised. "You'll not be surprised to learn the P.I. confirmed everything you've told us."

"Then why the big meeting?" Mercedes asked.

"I'm getting there. I've brought copies of the report, if anyone wants to see it. Basically it says that Spencer Ashton married Sally Barnett in Crawley, Nebraska, just as Grant said. She had twins a few months later, and he left her when the babies were a year old. Sally died when the children were twelve. Her parents raised them after that."

"And your point is?" Eli demanded. "None of this is news. Except maybe about Grant's mother dying when he was so young." He turned to Grant. "I'm sorry to hear that. I knew she was gone, but not that you were so young when it happened."

Grant nodded, a slight frown on his face as he watched Cole.

"There's something Grant left out, probably because he doesn't know it, either." Cole paused. "Spencer left Grant's mother forty-two years ago. He married our mother thirty-seven years ago. But he neglected to do one thing. He never got a divorce from his first wife."

In the sudden silence, Cole looked around the room at their faces—blank, shocked, disbelieving. "The detective checked very thoroughly. There is no record of a divorce."

"But—but this means…" Merry's voice trailed off.

"It means that our father's marriage to our mother was invalid. I have no idea where that leaves us in terms of the divorce settlement that gave him everything. Or," he added bleakly, "whether the surname listed on our birth certificates is correct. I don't know if we're Ashtons or not."

* * * * *

The secrets and scandals continue!
Abigail Ashton has come to Napa to meet
the family she never knew about. But it's
Russ Gannon, the foreman of Louret Vineyards,
who sends this feisty gal's heart reeling. The lone
wolf Russ knows that he isn't worthy of an
educated lady like Abby, but the fire when they
kiss tells another story!

Don't miss
A RARE SENSATION *by Kathie DeNosky,*
the second book in Silhouette Desire's
in-line continuity:
Dynasties: The Ashtons
Available February 2005.

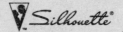

If you enjoyed what you just read,
then we've got an offer you can't resist!

Take 2 bestselling love stories FREE!

Plus get a FREE surprise gift!

Clip this page and mail it to Silhouette Reader Service™

IN U.S.A.
3010 Walden Ave.
P.O. Box 1867
Buffalo, N.Y. 14240-1867

IN CANADA
P.O. Box 609
Fort Erie, Ontario
L2A 5X3

YES! Please send me 2 free Silhouette Desire® novels and my free surprise gift. After receiving them, if I don't wish to receive anymore, I can return the shipping statement marked cancel. If I don't cancel, I will receive 6 brand-new novels every month, before they're available in stores! In the U.S.A., bill me at the bargain price of $3.80 plus 25¢ shipping and handling per book and applicable sales tax, if any*. In Canada, bill me at the bargain price of $4.47 plus 25¢ shipping and handling per book and applicable taxes**. That's the complete price and a savings of at least 10% off the cover prices—what a great deal! I understand that accepting the 2 free books and gift places me under no obligation ever to buy any books. I can always return a shipment and cancel at any time. Even if I never buy another book from Silhouette, the 2 free books and gift are mine to keep forever.

225 SDN DZ9F
326 SDN DZ9G

Name	(PLEASE PRINT)	
Address	Apt.#	
City	State/Prov.	Zip/Postal Code

Not valid to current Silhouette Desire® subscribers.

Want to try two free books from another series?
Call 1-800-873-8635 or visit www.morefreebooks.com.

* Terms and prices subject to change without notice. Sales tax applicable in N.Y.
** Canadian residents will be charged applicable provincial taxes and GST.
 All orders subject to approval. Offer limited to one per household.
 ® are registered trademarks owned and used by the trademark owner and or its licensee.

DES04R   ©2004 Harlequin Enterprises Limited

e**HARLEQUIN**.com

The Ultimate Destination for Women's Fiction

For **FREE online reading,** visit
www.eHarlequin.com now and enjoy:

Online Reads
Read **Daily** and **Weekly** chapters from
our Internet-exclusive stories by your
favorite authors.

Interactive Novels
Cast your vote to help decide how these
stories unfold...then stay tuned!

Quick Reads
For shorter romantic reads, try our
collection of Poems, Toasts, & More!

Online Read Library
Miss one of our online reads?
Come here to catch up!

Reading Groups
Discuss, share and rave with other
community members!

For great reading online,
visit www.eHarlequin.com today!

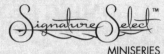

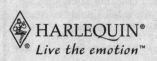

COMING NEXT MONTH

#1633 A RARE SENSATION—Kathie DeNosky
Dynasties: The Ashtons
Veterinarian Abigail Ashton wasn't looking to lose her virginity while
staying at Louret Vineyards—then again, she hadn't counted on meeting
sexy cowboy Russ Gannon. After a night of unexpected passion, Russ
assumed he wasn't Abby's kind of guy. Little did he know, he'd caused a
rare sensation that Abby didn't want to end.

#1634 HER MAN UPSTAIRS—Dixie Browning
Divas Who Dish
Marty Owens needed to remodel her home and asked handsome contractor
Cole Stevens for help, never guessing their heated debates would turn
into heated passion with one thing leading to another…and another….
Yet Marty knew that the higher she flew the harder she'd fall, and
wondered if her heart could handle falling for the man upstairs.

#1635 BREATHLESS PASSION—Emilie Rose
The only son of North Carolina's wealthiest family, stunningly sexy
Rick Faulkner needed Lily West's help. Before long, their platonic
relationship turned into white-hot passion, and now Lily, a girl from
the wrong side of the tracks, wanted her Cinderella story to last forever….

#1636 OUT OF UNIFORM—Amy J. Fetzer
Marine captain Rick Wyatt and his wife, Kate, were great together—skin
to skin. But beyond the bedroom door, Rick closed Kate out emotionally,
and she wanted in. When an injury forced Rick out of uniform, Kate
passionately set out to win the battle for her marriage.

#1637 A SINGLE DEMAND—Margaret Allison
Cassie Edwards had gone to a tropical resort to meet with corporate raider
Steve Axon but ended up losing her virginity to a sexy bartender instead.
Then Cassie returned home to a surprise: her bartender *was* Steve Axon!
Mixing business with pleasure was not part of her plan and Cassie was
determined to forget that night—but Steve had another demand….

#1638 BOUGHT BY A MILLIONAIRE—Heidi Betts
Chicago's Most Eligible Bachelor, millionaire Burke Bishop, wanted a
child and hired Shannon Moriarity to have his baby. Knowing that Burke
would make a wonderful father, Shannon had agreed to keep things strictly
business—but soon she realized Burke would make the perfect husband.
But would Mr. Anti-Marriage agree to Shannon's change of terms?